D1116605

THE LUNATICS OF TERRA

By the same author

BLACK ALICE
(with Thomas M. Disch)
THE REPRODUCTIVE SYSTEM
THE MÜLLER-FOKKER EFFECT
THE STEAM-DRIVEN BOY
THE NEW APOCRYPHA
KEEP THE GIRAFFE BURNING
BLACK AURA
INVISIBLE GREEN
RODERICK
RODERICK AT RANDOM
ALIEN ACCOUNTS
TIK-TOK

THE LUNATICS OF TERRA

by

John Sladek

LONDON
VICTOR GOLLANCZ LTD
1984

British Library Cataloguing in Publication Data
Sladek, John
The lunatics of Terra.
I. Title
813'.54[F] PS3569.L25

ISBN 0-575-03464-5

Printed in Great Britain by
St Edmundsbury Press Ltd, Bury St Edmunds, Suffolk

Contents

The Last of the Whaleburgers

When Chad Link came home from work early and found his wife in another man's arms, he asked the obvious question: Where was the other man?

"I see this pair of arms here, Daffodil, but I don't see no owner."

"I can explain."

"Sure, sure. You can explain anything. It's your job." He turned to the bar and ordered synthetic scotch with real water. "I suppose this guy is a meat person?"

"That's none of your business, Chad. Under Section 27 of our marriage contract, clause 8—"

"Fine!" He slammed down the empty glass and ordered another drink. But the bar, which knew Chad, ignored the order.

"Anyway," said Daffodil, "I'm not ready with that answer. I thought you were going to ask me how long this has been going on."

"Okay, how long has this been going on?"

"Two years, three months, seventeen days, five hours, twenty-three minutes and seven-point-nine seconds, that's up to the time I thought you were going to ask. You want to know why?"

"You don't have to coach me on *every* question, Daff." On *Dorinda's Destiny*, the world's longest-running soap opera, a character might at this point turn away to gaze out a window. There were no windows here, but Chad wheeled around to face the wall. "Why, Daff? *Why?*"

She waited until he wheeled back to face her. "It's all your fault."

"My fault?"

The vertical rows of tear-lights on her cheeks energized, indicating a copious flow of emotion. "You had to be one of those people who takes a job away from home. Nobody goes out to work these days, nobody but you. Why, Flopsy Doubloon has a hubby who never sets foot out of the house!"

"Of course not, how could he?" Burt Doubloon had himself built into the wall over the fireplace, like a full-size portrait. "They can only have sex by hologram, is that what you want?"

"Sex isn't everything." She extended her real foot. "Do you think I need an instep tattoo? Yumyum says they have these new scented floral——"

"You can sit there in another guy's arms and say sex isn't everything?"

"Don't try to change the subject. We were talking about your so-called job. Demonstrating dinner, that's degrading. It's really degrading."

Chad thought of trying the bar again. "Oh, *now* you tell me. I spend years working my way up—demonstrating drinks, canapés, snacks, breakfasts, light lunches, business picnics. *Now*, when I'm up to full dinners, the peak of my career, *now* you suddenly decide it's degrading. Well I got news for you: I like this here job and I'm good at it. It just so happens that people pay plenty to see me demonstrate."

"Look, I've heard all this before. People pay plenty, they come from all over the world——"

"They do. Chinese oil tycoons, the crowned heads of Europe, video stars, the Czar of Prussia——"

"Russia."

"Russia, Prussia, wherever. The point is, this Czar came halfway around the world just to watch me crush a grape against the roof of my mouth, and why? Because I take pride in my work. I use genuine food, whole food. I don't crush half a grape. Yes and when I bite into a whaleburger, they can all see and smell how real it is. And they pay plenty."

"Money isn't everything, either."

"Tell me what is?"

At that moment, their voices were lost in the high-density sound emitted by their four walls, while the room itself was lost in brilliant images flickering from every surface. The room said:

Going out? Gee, that's expensive.

Staying in? Aw, that's boring.

But hey, why not go out at home?—with VI-CAR! VI-CAR, the vicarious vehicle for busy stay-at-homes, gives you everything. Why miss out on the speed, the thrills, the spills, the quiet reflective moments in traffic jams, the hammer-down exhilaration of real high-performance mobility? With VI-CAR, you don't have to go out to drive!

For a moment or two they sat, stunned, their ears buzzing and their eyes slowly readjusting to life again. Chad and Daff were getting used to home commercials, but Wendell crouched in the corner and whimpered. Wendell was their chimpanion.

Chad picked up the thread of conversation: "Why, Daff? *Why?*"

"Because you don't think of me as a woman any more."

Strictly speaking, Daffodil Link wasn't a woman any more. Except for her foot and fingerprints, all of her visible parts had been replaced with improvements made of metal, high-quality plastics and mahogany.

"Sure I do," he said, without conviction. Strictly speaking, Chad Link wasn't a man any more, either. He'd begun life as a 90% meat product, but accidents, wear-and-tear and preventative maintenance had reduced him to a brain hemisphere and one elbow—or was it one eyebrow? The hemisphere kept forgetting.

"Why did we ever get married in the first place?" Daffodil asked, moving to the next logical question.

"We got married, as I recall, because a computer said we were compatible in a hundred ways: same life goals, same ideas of work enrichment, same marketing impact preferences. . . ."

"It was a very old computer, Chad. Let's face it, our marriage has reached a probabilistically critical disjuncture."

"Only if you use Reverend Bunky's Statistical Marriage Therapy System," he said. "I happen to prefer the Ghee Bagwash system of Transcendental Number Therapy, and I say we've reached an old-fashioned Number 8 crisis."

"That's what I mean, we don't even talk the same marriage therapy language."

"You mean that's what *I* mean."

"No, Chad, if I meant what you mean, we wouldn't have a problem."

"Exactly."

"Q.E.D."

"Right."

This agreement (itself a Number 7 crisis) might have gone on forever, but once more the walls exploded in light and sound:

The last six minutes of life have been brought to you by Burve, the Instant Food Shine.

Harriet, boomed one wall, *how do you get your food so darned shiny? I use a food shine myself, but I never get anything like this. Why, you can see your face in that lentil weep! And your underbread—gleaming!*

Oh it's easy, Irma, yelped the opposite wall. Waves of sound passed through their bodies. The deafness of most consumers was taken for granted now, and the aim was for visceral listening. Their souls shook. *One drop of Burve can transform the refractive index of the dullest stew.*

Is that good?

See for yourself! You know, Irma, there are a lot of food shines around, but nothing like Burve. I keep an extra can in the bedroom and one in the bathroom—you never know!

When they recovered, the front door was welcoming their friends and neighbors, Luke and Yumyum Mangor.

"Hi, kids," said Luke.

"Love that front door," said Yumyum. It was a new door with extra features, including a combined playroom and decontamination chamber, panels of baked-on red enamel, and a sophisticated welcoming system involving the brains of fifteen sparrows.

"Great," said Luke. "Especially when it showed us these holograms of women stroking their own legs, laughing babies playing with puppies, and the flag flying over a Thanksgiving dinner, and finishing off with a flaming car crash."

Chad said, "All tested stuff, supposed to make you feel welcome. But do you think red enamel——?"

The Mangors assured him that red enamel was a perfect

choice, not only popular but distinguished. "It won the American Book Award this year," said Yumyum, "for best color."

Luke nodded. "It was up against blue and green, tough competition. Oh hello there, Wendell." The chimpanion took their coats and repair kits and carried them away.

"He'll search your coats for fleas," Daff said. "Poor Wendell! He just can't understand that there aren't any more fleas, anywhere."

"You like him," Yumyum said. "Have you ever thought of adopting him?"

Chad said, "They turned us down."

There was a short silence, before Daffodil said: "Maybe if we didn't have children of our own, maybe they'd let us adopt Wendell." There was a long silence.

Children aren't everything, Chad thought, remembering when he and Daff had last gone to visit the children. Only one visit a year was allowed, and even for that the parents had to wear protective clothing, stand behind concrete walls and fondle the children by means of remote mechanical hands. The kids, little Ford and Chrysanthemum, seemed happy enough. They spent a lot of their time playing hide-and-go-seek in the dark with other kids. They all glowed beautifully.

"And they say the art of conversation is dead," Yumyum was about to remark, when the next commercial came up and wiped their minds clean.

"Have you seen today's opinion poll?" Yumyum finally asked. "President Punch is up again after that terrible slump when he criticized daytime TV."

"They never learn," said Daffodil. "There are some things even a president can't get away with criticizing. Look what happened to President Spot."

"What did happen?" said Luke.

"Don't you remember? He said that any organized religion that helps people commit suicide is going too far. Well, you know how that went down with the Church of Jeepers Creepers—gosh, their sacrament is cyanide. Naturally they went to work on him, and in no time at all, his share was down to point-oh-nine! They never learn."

Chad opined that you can't teach an old dog new tricks.

Luke objected that Spot, a three-year-old cocker spaniel, hadn't been that old.

Yumyum wondered if electing animals to office hadn't been a mistake all along.

"There's always been a lot of controversy about it," Daff explained. "Though strictly speaking, we elect the animals' owners. But the Supreme Court ruled that you can't prevent an owner—especially of a famous movie dog like Spot—from using his animal's publicity value in a campaign. Of course some people objected to a president who has to have burrs combed out of his ears. But the fact is, most people trust animals."

"You sure know a lot," said Luke.

Chad chuckled. "It's her job. Daff is an encyclopedia therapist. Helps people solve their problems by explaining facts to them. Go on, ask her anything."

But Daffodil had not yet finished. "The controversy deepened last year when Punch became the first puppet elected to our highest office. The character 'Punch' has been with us for many centuries, by the way, as part of a traditional puppet show called 'Punch and Judy'. But ten years ago the Yxar Corporation made the name and character part of its trademark, used on everything from character toys to smart weapons. To popularize the Punch theme, Yxar's marketing people hit on the novel idea of running Punch for president. Punch's election was a landslide, indicating that most people trust objects even more than animals. Now the name stands for freedom and justice, for quality products from the Yxar family of companies, where caring and sharing count. Any questions?"

"How do you keep talking so long?" Yumyum asked. "It's like one of those you know video documentaries where this narrator talks for maybe two whole minutes at a time."

Luke nodded. "Like when they explain the vast dark distances between the stars or the psychology of spiders."

They sat for awhile in silence, as though contemplating the vast dark, the spiders. Yumyum looked around for something new.

"Is that a new kardio-pump?" she asked, and picked up the elegant little jeweled gadget. With its tiny, gleaming crank, it looked a little like an old-fashioned meat grinder. "All mechanical?"

"We got it in Venice," Chad said. "Go on, try it out."

"Hey, great!" Luke plugged it into his chest port and turned the crank. As the pump moved blood through his body, its tinkling chimes played *Stranger in Paradise*.

"Great!" he said. Daffodil's eyes glowed with a steady, three-candlepower light, and the blush-light in Chad's cheek energized.

"How was Venice?"

Chad said, "Terrific, they've got some terrific games there. You don't even need to leave the airport, just go right into your hotel game rooms. Well, we did go out once to see the sunken city. Real impressive. See, they preserved it all in plastic down there under the water, and they built in lights, streaker lights, dazzlers, holograms—so it's like a great big game table. Outstanding."

All at once, Daffodil said, "Our marriage is breaking down."

"What?" asked the visitors together.

"I said our marriage is breaking down."

Luke laughed. "I thought you said your marriage *counsellor* was breaking down. That's what happened to us last week, didn't it, Yum?"

"I'll say. He came to see us and got stuck on the doorstep. All of a sudden there was all this smoke coming out of his ankles and you could hear motors screaming inside."

Luke laughed again. "Then he just fell over sideways, and his sample case broke open. Man, there were all these dozens of vibrators bouncing all over the place, shaped like everything from dumbbells to Oscars, and all these funny clothes, leather and chains, gingham aprons and barbecue sets, you name it."

"It made us realize," Yumyum said, "how pointless it all was. I mean, we tried everything, over the years. Therapy, counselling, sports. We had children, we adopted children, we adopted animals. We lived apart, lived together, divorced, remarried, you name it."

"You name it," Luke agreed. "So finally we decided to join the Jeepers Creepers."

Daffodil gasped. "You're going to kill yourselves?"

"We prefer to call it discorporating. And you know, it really makes all the difference. All of a sudden, life is—what's the word?—*good*. Life is *good*," Luke said.

"We're content," added his bride.

Chad shook his head. "Well, pardon me, but death is something I really don't approve of. I can't even watch that terrible game show, what do they call it? *Lay It on the Line*. Where the losers get vaporized."

"Don't be so bloody negative," Luke said. "That's a good show."

Yumyum said, "The point is, all marriages are doomed. It's an archaic institution. Okay for its time, way back say in 1950, but not relevant to today's needs. Today's world doesn't need weddings, it needs funerals. Too many people, not enough happiness. Marriage can't adapt, so it's doomed."

"Before long, it'll be extinct," Luke said. "They'll probably put the last married couple in a museum, alongside the last whaleburger."

Next day, Daff and Chad drove out to see the kids. An attendant looked at their passes. "I'm real sorry, folks, you can't have a regular visit today. Not for another four months."

"What if it was kind of an emergency?" Daffodil asked.

"Real sorry. Regulations." The attendant bowed its head in thought for a moment. "I guess I could let you go up on the observation deck. You might be able to see your little Ford and Chrysanthemum from there, if they're out playing."

There were a few other parents on the observation deck, some at the huge window, some resting from the view. An old man was sitting with his back to the view, watching an old-fashioned fireside TV with the sound up loud. They heard the brassy theme music for *Lay It on the Line*.

The view was panoramic. The entire camp, with its double fences and little gray huts, lay spread out below. A few children were playing among the huts, but none looked like Ford or Chrysanthemum.

And here's our genial host, Mel Mowbray! brayed the television, at their backs. *Thank you. Good evening folks, time to* Lay It on the Line. *Now you know the rules: We start with twenty wonderful couples, and we end up with one winning couple. The losers get these Beautiful Delvaux hand-crafted coffins and all expense-paid funerals from Delvaux of Hollywood! The winner gets ONE BILLION DOLLARS! Now what do you say? Ready to play?*

Why couldn't life be like a game? Chad wondered. Or like a 1950 TV comedy where all the misunderstandings get cleared up in the last minute?

Beyond the camp, it seemed as if they could see the whole world. On the left, there was the freeway that had brought them from the city. They could even see the detour (where a mantle of fungus was eating the concrete).

"The sun's going down," Daffodil said.

On the right they could see a distant suburb burning. Overhead was the usual layer of brown haze. Half a dozen helicopters were churning through it, carrying between them what seemed to be a dead whale.

From time to time the TV gave out a raucous buzz. At each buzz a contestant was eliminated. The TV audience usually gasped, sometimes laughed nervously.

"I think I'd rather live," she said suddenly.

Chad felt close to her. Closer than the shave you get with the all-new Sforza razor, 8192 tiny blades to whirl the whiskers away. Closer even than Hypno-spray, the shower that cleans your mind while it cleans your body. He felt as though they were both being penetrated by rays of some incredible purity, light of a new and exciting quality. It was a 1950 cathode ray.

"Forget those arms," he said. "I don't care whose they were."

"They were yours. I got them for your birthday."

"My birthday!"

Brassy theme music swelled behind them. They stood at the window, arms around one another, until it was too dark to tell one kid from another. They were all just so many tiny, glowing figures, dancing about like fireflies.

AFTERWORD

I wrote this not long after my own marriage broke up in 1982. Not being sure whether to think of separation as a mortal defeat or simply a recovery from double vision, I tried reading a few of the many books on the subject. Usually these turned out to be interviews with people who, by their own accounts, were victims. They'd all had plenty to put up with: flagrant philandering, Gestapo tortures, compulsive gambling or drinking, desertion, attempted murder or suicide.

Somehow all these confessions of Bluebeard's ex-wives and Manon's ex-husbands didn't seem relevant to our case. My wife and I didn't hate each other or even dislike each other. Neither of us was a victim, and neither was behaving insanely. We were just tired of being married to us. Why? I read on.

Like many others (especially like A. Alvarez) I tried looking for some universal truth in this personal catastrophe. Wasn't marriage itself becoming an anachronism? Couldn't history be somehow blamed? Or how about blaming statistics? With one-third of all British, and one-half of all American marriages failing, what chance for an Anglo-American marriage?

Finally I decided to stop scouring the writings of others for an answer and write one out myself. The answer to all modern marriage problems, I've decided, is to return to the wonderful Fifties, when men were men (and had suits with padded shoulders to prove it) and women were hostesses. In those days, you couldn't even see a movie about divorce. Any movie which showed a man and woman going into the courthouse together was permissible only if they weren't married. Even then they had to go into separate courtrooms. And if a woman was shown boarding a plane, it had to be made clear that she was not *going to Reno.*

Alas, that golden age is gone. Even the President of the United States is a grass widower. Britain, though it has not yet sunk to that depth, is on the way—it has a Prime Minister who is clearly a female impersonator, and no doubt a divorcé is next.

If I've said it once, I've said it a thousand times (and vice versa): we must strive to return to those days of innocence. It would be a start if we could put the lead back into petrol, resume atmospheric testing of nuclear weapons, and of course bring back capital punishment. When those small steps have given us confidence, we can move on to greater steps like the Korean War, black-and-white television and finally, no divorce.

Great Mysteries Explained!

Science no longer confines itself to answering the kind of question no one ever asks ("But tell me, how *do* slime molds communicate?"). Instead, scientists are emerging from their stuffy labs into the real world, to tackle a few real-life mysteries:

1. **Who killed Kennedy?** The Dealey Plaza demise remains the number-one mystery of our age. The Warren Commission concluded only that Kennedy was shot by one person using one bullet, or by several persons using several bullets, but probably not by several persons sharing the same bullet. But this leaves many unanswered questions:

Was Lee Harvey Oswald in the Texas Book Depository merely to deposit a Texas Book? What of the FBI? The CIA? The Better Business Bureau? Could the President have conceivably been cleaning a gun in his car at the time?

Demographers may try a fresh approach to the problem: Since *everyone in the world remembers where he or she was at the moment the shot was fired*, why not put all those alibis into one computer and check them out? Careful cross-checking could eliminate billions of suspects and narrow it down to one or two persons who remember being in Dealey Plaza with rifles.

2. **Is the Turin shroud genuine?** Light may be shed on this mystery by the recent discovery of a similar relic, the Neapolitan shroud. This is very like the Turin object, but comes in three colors. Tourists maintain it is the burial shroud of Christ; skeptics insist it is an old beach towel.

Science at first did little to help resolve the controversy. Carbon-14 tests established its date as A.D. 1953 ± 18 million years. X-ray analysis showed the shroud to have an abcess in an upper left incisor that needs immediate attention. For chemical analysis one corner was removed and the remainder burnt—revealing it to be woven of some kind of fiber.

The big breakthrough was the discovery of a curious symbol on the surviving corner. Scholars now believe it is the authentic laundry mark of Joseph of Arimathea. Tough luck, Turin.

3. **Can human beings be cloned?** Some journalists claim certain rich men are hiring biologists to clone them. Other journalists think clones are pointy cylinders.

A clone is an exact genetic replica of someone, reared in a test tube and therefore somewhat sensitive to the sound of breaking glass. A clone gets all of his or her chromosomes from one parent, as well as all of his or her allowance. Clones who develop Oedipal problems have only themselves to blame.

Why should rich men go around cloning themselves? First, there are tax advantages in claiming yourself as hundreds of dependents. Clones can sign your checks, answer your phone and break in new shoes, and perform hundreds of other services before they break down with an acute identity crisis. (Psychiatrists will soon encounter a new syndrome, *cloneliness*.)

Responsible geneticists pooh-pooh the idea. Carrot clones, yes. Frogs, maybe. Humans? Pooh-pooh. There are insuperable technical problems, such as how to make very large test tubes.

But what if they are wrong? What if thousands of Howard Hughes clones are hiding away in Las Vegas hotel rooms?

What if China develops a clone weapon—a phalanx of waiters *who look exactly alike*—to cause the final confusion and collapse of the decadent West?

What if the Osmonds . . . ? But enough speculation. "The rich," Scott Fitzgerald said to Ernest Hemingway, "are not like you and me." Soon the rich may be exactly like everybody—only more so.

4. **Is there intelligent life anywhere in the universe?** The great UFO debate began in 1947 when a retired army major, flying over the Cascade mountains, saw a group of strange objects flying in formation. He circled for a closer look and saw that they were geese. He did not report this unusual experience for fear of being branded a hoaxer or a lunatic. Later someone else

reported seeing Faust in Hell; a reporter's mishearing of "frying sorcerer" made world headlines.

Suddenly everyone saw things in the sky: A Navy pilot saw baskets of peaches over Alaska. Four boy scouts saw a flying tickertape machine that turned into a chicken salad sandwich without mayonnaise. One police chief chased a saucer for two hours, but failed to get its license number. Elsewhere saucers caused cars to run out of gas, and stole underwear off clotheslines.

Finally the Air Force promised to investigate all sightings of "uninteresting flying objects", or UFOs. Their report, now declassified, breaks down sightings into several categories: meteorites, mirages, hoaxes, Wedgwood, etc. There remains at bottom a tiny residue of saucer cases that cannot be eliminated (not to be confused with the residue in the bottoms of saucers, which you can eliminate with baking soda: soak one hour and scrub). For instance:

Mr A, 73, watched a bright light descend and land on his lawn sprinkler. Ten tiny George Washingtons leapt out, bound him hand and foot, and forced him to eat a magnetized pizza.

Mr B, 12, took the only known clear, detailed movie of a saucer, showing a large complex structure with portholes, flaming jets, colored lights and an upper deck on which naked aliens could be seen playing shuffleboard. But the drugstore refused to develop this film.

The Air Force will soon declassify evidence confirming that UFOs are from space. Aliens have for centuries been trying to contact us, probably to borrow money. They travel the galaxy in a mother ship. Smaller craft descend to explore our planet, remaining below until the mother ship tells them to come back up and wash their hands for dinner.

Afterword

This first appeared in Isaac Asimov's Science Fiction Magazine.

While I have never met Isaac Asimov, I suspect that we agree entirely about the value of pseudoscience: that it's good for a laugh.

Being a scientist as well as a science fiction writer, Dr Asimov would of course have two reasons for opposing pseudoscience. Counterfeit science devalues the currency of real science, just as bad money drives out good. People who become convinced that Velikovsky's astronomy is just as good (or as bad) as Newton's astronomy, or that Biblical Creationism is just as scientific as evolution, are heading for intellectual bankruptcy.

But sf writers also have a grudge against pseudoscience, namely that it's poaching in our stream without a license. While sf writers work at producing ideas, wishes, dreams and inventions to entertain and edify, all their work is carefully labelled Fiction. Yes, we all want to meet intelligent visitors from another planet face to face, we all want to possess superhuman powers like telepathy and psychokinesis and precognition, and we all want there to be ape-men on Everest and a dragon in Loch Ness. But we are able to distinguish between the wishes of Fiction and the facts of real life.

Pseudoscience is not so careful about labelling. Often (as with Erich von Däniken) science fiction ideas are simply lifted wholesale and presented as fact. Likewise the story of a child encountering a flying saucer, which has been circulating in sf magazines for decades, turns up in Uri Geller's autobiography. Most "true" UFO stories bear an amazing resemblance to earlier sf stories. Hence the haunting familiarity of Steven Spielberg's sf films: They are science fiction based on "true" accounts which are in turn based on science fiction.

Red Noise

Like for example there was this old party with a lot of hair in his nose Mel his name was Mel Hankers, real old time country shit-kicker, you remember him? From way back, he used to do *Walkin the Floor over You* a lotta crap like that, I remember he was cuttin this album and we was all goin nuts on this one number, tried it about fifty times and he never got it right, never. *Red Roses for a Blue Lady*, he kept missing his cue or coughing stammering or some goddam thing. And all that hair in his nose I started wantin to do a little heart surgery, you know? But anyway finally he got up and picked up this shoebox and went to the can and we all thought uh huh what is it a bottle or a kit or what, and he comes back, picks up his guitar and cuts the track in one take, no problem. So we all get curious, coupla guys make bets, so I hafta go get the shoebox and look in it. It was a squashed frog, all bleeding and squirming around in that box, and that's just one example.

If Wally was here he could tell you, Wally's real deep, a real thinker. Wally says it all started with some Greek who invented the harp, way back when. Apollo his name was, and he got in some kinda music contest, against this flute-player. Apollo won, and guess what first prize was? He got to have the other guy skinned alive. For real, and they nailed the skin to a tree. Wally says if music be the food of hate, let's take it from the second ending, he says a lot of weird stuff. If I listened good to everything he says I'd either be rich or dead. The food of hate though I like that, that's real deep. But I was gonna tell you about Encores Unlimited.

It all started the day after Aldo Heartsock snuffed it, remember? Yeah I guess everybody remembers where they was that day. We was sittin around inna office and everybody was gettin real depressed, real deep depressed. Because whether you like the guy or not, and personally I feel I could do without some of that Heartsock's Peace garbage, I mean life is just too short. Okay maybe I'm wrong okay it's just my opinion frankly that Peace people oughta be sterilized with a chain saw, okay maybe I'm wrong but it's a free country. Anyway like I say you may not like the guy but you gotta respect him. You gotta see his death as a great loss, like I figure it lost us about forty-six million dollars, I mean us at Volute Records. Sure I know everybody thinks record companies *like* dead artists, and I admit that a wild fantastic death like Aldo's makes a good hump in the old sales curve, but like they say, when the hump is over, everybody's sad. People forget dead artists, because they don't cut no new sides.

Okay there we are, sittin around in the Volute Records office, and I said, Wally, that's what really hurts, we don't get no more new stuff. Aldo's dead now, just like Elvis. A thing of the past.

Wally says, Of course you can't compare his death with Elvis's, that was straightforward, a guy just walked up to him and emptied a .38 into him—

That wasn't Elvis, that was John Lennon, I said. It just proves how people forget. They'll forget Aldo too, just because he was eaten by alligators inside his private plane don't mean people will remember him any more than they remember the fan who laid those gators on him.

Torn to pieces by admirers, Wally says to himself. Just like Orpheus. And then he starts telling me another long, drawn-out story about this Apollo who this time is the sun, and this Orpheus is a priest at his temple, he sings and plays the harp pretty good. Only these women hear him and go nuts and tear him to pieces. They throw his head in the river and it floats down to the sea, still singing. Wally asks me what that story means to me.

I say I don't know, but if this Apollo is the sun that explains how he peeled the skin off that other guy.

Wally says, No I just meant, the singing doesn't stop when Orpheus dies. I wonder if we couldn't do that for Aldo—keep him singing?

I don't know what he's got in his mind, Wally's deep as shit. I say, Resurrection ain't exactly my line a work, I'm just a humble co-creative production adviser. To me, dead is dead. Maybe you got a difference of opinion or something, it's a free country.

Well when Wally Barnes gets one a these ideas he gets glassy-eyed and stops listening, you know? After awhile he says, You know that retake machine we got, why can't we work something out with that?

He means this synthesizing computer we got for when a artist screws up too many times in a session, you use this instead of retakes, I guess what it does is something with digital recording, it kind of fakes the artist's voice for a bar or two doing what we want, and we can dub that fake piece in. And you wouldn't believe how fucked up some a these artists are when they come in to record, we have to fake a lot but they still get all the credit. Like the big heart-throb club singer Grant Tormey, puked all the way through the session, brought up more puke than notes, you know?

Wally says why not kind of extend this machine some way, and have it do a whole side by itself? Because in that case you wouldn't even need a live artist.

I don't get it but Wally says Leave it to me. You just leave the thinking to me, Red. You take care of the sleeve notes and leave the thinking to me.

I say great Wally, thinking how would he like it if somebody sewed his right eyeball to his left nut and stuff like that. But whether you like the guy or not you gotta respect him he's real deep, a thinker.

So anyway he starts having these conferences with all these weird engineer types, you know the kinda guys if you Nice Day em they gotta work it out on their computer before they Nice Day you back. Some of em even wear glasses, over-the-ears *glasses* for christ sake, if we let em they'd probably show up for work in neckties too. Well almost every day there's one or two of these jerks in the office flapping their jaws not that Wally understands it any more than me, most of the time they talk to themselves.

Wally kept tryina tell me what was pulling off only he didn't know nothin, a lot of crap about hitches and glitches, phrase expectation number and shit like that. What he did say though was how they was gonna start with a kind of voice print and then add all kinds a stuff like expression and how the singer gets into a note and how he breathes. And maybe in the case of Aldo Heartsock they would dub in hiccups he used to get em before every session.

Well some a these guys wanted to start out with a pure voice, a standard voice they could fool around with, twiddle some knobs on it an get it like they wanted. The other guys wanted to build up each voice from scratch, I never did find out who won, who got their hide nailed to the tree, ha ha.

I was personally pretty fuckin busy about that time as co-creative production adviser I hadda take this camera crew out and make sure they got some real nasty shots of some real nasty streets for this new album *Greaseburger Kill* by Harriet and the Horsedorks. Like if you leave it to them they go all the safe places and you end up with shit like maybe a brick wall with one dirty word on it, you might as well use a studio. No I took em where they could squat down behind a real dead body, beautiful you can't compare nothing to that, a bum with a knife hangin outa his throat lying there with his eyes open. And the guy who killed him is hanging around waitin for us to go so he can get his blade back, that's the kinda neighborhood it was, and that was only the start, we also went to the *real* nasty streets where the bums get set on fire . . . all this took a lot of time but it was worth it just to give the album visual guts for all the nice people who never get a chance to rip each other, they really go for this stuff like they used to go for public executions. I get to thinkin about this one day on one real nasty street, about what Wally said how music feeds on blood.

Wally says the Aztecs used to pick out some kid and make him a kind of god or something, give him a big party with all the food and booze and women he wanted for days and days until the time comes to pay the bill you might say. They get him drunk one last time and they dress him in this human skin because that's how this god likes to dress up. And they make him walk through the streets playing these clay flutes, to the big pyramid. Then he climbs up the pyramid and he breaks the clay flutes and leaves them behind him, and when he gets to the top there's the priest with this obsidian blade who chops his heart out, Wally says. And Wally says they put the heart in a alabaster box.

Well I'm thinking all this over while I walk through them nasty streets, like how come flutes all the time in them stories, how come people get their skin peeled off all the time? I'm thinkin so hard I get cut off from the camera team I'm in the warehouse districk and I'm on my own, nobody else in the street. Just me and all them big dirty buildins, dirty brick and maybe cast iron on the front lookin like I don't know frozen music, you know?

Then I see I'm not alone, on the steps a this one place between the big cast iron columns here's this wino sleeping it off. I go up close to take a look and I see he's got a lot of hair in his nose just like old Mel Hankers. Then the sonofabitch turns over and farts in my face and I hear him groaning *Red Roses for a Blue Lady*—the sonofabitch *is* Mel Hankers!

The empty wine bottle is by his feet, I grab it and smash it on one cast iron column. I get ready to cut the old bastard's throat only—god damn it, I got to see if he sings that damn song all the way through, you know? I mean he never could sing it before without a mistake, but now here he was half-conscious but singin it, I hadda wait and see. I waited, but then the camera team come around the corner so I never get the chance to kill that bastard with all that hair in his nose. He's probably in some derelick bar right now, him and that hair singing *Walkin the Floor over You*. I felt real bad the rest of the day, not getting my chance to rip his skin.

Next day Wally says the new machine is ready. All of us go to this old recording studio now half full of computer cabinets, with all them engineering types crawlin around on top of them or under them, passing each other wires and reading charts and whatever, all of em got *glasses* and one has a *pipe*, for christ sake. All of a sudden somebody says sshh, and Wally pushes buttons and out comes this voice singin in Kraut. They all get real excited, but it don't sound like much to me. It turns out that the song is by Schubert something about a trout Wally says. And the singer is Elvis.

I see this is supposed to surprise shit out of me so I say so what, you found some old tape?

Nope. Elvis never recorded Schubert's *Die Forelle*, says Wally, looking deep. We made it all up: voice and all!

A guy with glasses butts in, saying the hardest part was patching in the German pronunciation, they hadda work from some record this Elvis did, *Bei mir bist Du schön*, it was harder than doing a skin graft without skin. I am wondering why he said that, but then Wally and this guy start explaining stuff to me I can't understand.

After all, says the guy, music isn't spiritual, it's made by physical vibrations in air. We can synthesize a human voice or a crumhorn or a flute just the same. We work up the voice of somebody dead and gone, and we get them to cut a new record. In the future—

I'm all in favor of the future, I said, but if you'll excuse me all to hell, this sounds like robbin graves.

It is, Wally says and grins. We make the dead rise up in their graves and sing, sing, sing! Did I mention Wally shoves a lot of coke up his nose sometimes? He was talkin on and on about how we could get Charlie Parker to open up a hundred new solos not just on alto but soprano and tenor and sopranino, sure and why not Paderewski on the accordion?

Anyway Red, he finished, it's up to you now. You gotta sell this little package to the public, better write some press releases. We're changing the name of the company from Volute to—listen to this—*Encores Unlimited*. Can you handle that?

I swallow my gum and get busy at the old word box, pretty soon I come up with this:

ENCORES UNLIMITED

For John Lennon, it was five .38 slugs from a madman's gun. For Jimi Hendrix it was an H too big. For Buddy Holly it was an accident, for Bessie Smith it was Southern inhospitality. And what about Judy Garland, Mahalia Jackson, Jennie Tourel, Janis Joplin? What about Enrico Caruso and John

McCormack? Gone, and gone forever. The world is poorer without them.

Gone? Are they? A revolutionary system devised by Wallace Barnes of Volute Records promises "encores unlimited". So confident is Barnes that he's changing the name of his company. From now on, the company will be called *Encores Unlimited.*

"It's an entirely new process," says Barnes. "It enables us to bring dead artists back to life, to record brand new numbers—a dream come true."

But just how does the Encores Unlimited process work? It begins with a digital recording of any artist doing any number at all. The computer is programmed to make an exhaustive search over this material for "patterns".

Which patterns? That's still a trade secret, but Barnes says "everything is considered, from the single note on up. The computer program asks how each note is delivered, examines it for pitch, stress, intonation, volume, harmonic color, duration, all the things that make the artist unique.

"Of course that's just at the simplest level," Barnes added. "We also have to look at the composition. Our computer program in a sense subtracts the music from the voice—leaving style without content. First we have to catch on to a thousand little tricks of the performer, how he or she interprets intervals, gets into a pure pitch and so on. We put all this into larger and larger patterns. And the largest pattern *is* the performer."

Asked how a computer can simulate a whole personality, Barnes explained, "The computer has to get inside the head of the artist, sensing in advance what he or she is going to do next before he does it, in advance, prior to any action, beforehand, anticipating what he's going to do before he does it, ahead of time. Like if a computer word processor was able to see what I was going to say next and come in first with, 'What I was going to say next and come in first with, "Come in first" or something' or something like that."

The process works on any artist on record. Encores Unlimited has plans galore! Chaliapin (d. 1938) will be made to sing

Folsom Prison for a change of image; likewise Judy Garland (d. 1969) singing Andalusian folk songs and Jimi Hendrix playing new arrangements of Sousa marches—while John Philip Sousa and his Marine Band play Hendrix. Will Buddy Holly and Billie Holiday perform *Billy Budd*? Will Caruso try *Carousel*? Anything is possible. We may soon hear those famous "sweethearts", Jeanette MacDonald (d. 1965) and Nelson Eddy (d. 1967) getting together again to record their version of the new hit rock musical, *Manson!*

First off we get a lot of trouble outa other record companies and certain critics, a lot of talk about Wally bein a ghoul robbin graves desecratin memories and then some critics try to make out that our stuff is terrible, nothing like the originals, other critics say maybe we got some old pirate tapes. Nobody likes us but the public. They can't get enough of our stuff, the first year we never get caught up with orders. That pisses off a lot of live artists—second-rate bums—whose sales are goin down. There's talk about lobbying for a law against us, even, but all that don't make no difference, Encores Unlimited just keeps smashing through. By the end a the year *Fortune* is mentioning this "Whiz-kid Wallace Barnes" and *New Yorker* has a cartoon of our office, with a guy in a white dinner jacket sayin to a computer, "Play Sam again, 'It'." We figure next thing will be a cover of *Time*.

Everything is goin fine, so naturally Wally is gettin bored. Like always he wants to fuck around with some new idea, he wants to carry everything too far.

He starts talkin again about music and violence, how you can't have good music without blood and death. He calls this the red noise, it's there in real music but not in our Encores Unlimited stuff. Because, he says, computers don't know how it feels to murder.

Who does, I ask, but he's not listening. Now he's yakkin on about the lower brain or the right side brain and how maybe the part that makes music is the killer shark beneath the surface of the mind—anyway the bottom line is, the reason we like music so much is because we don't get a chance to butcher each other no more.

So he wanted to do this experiment using maybe a human being for a computer. Like put headphones on somebody, and feed him the sound of a nasty murder while he plays or sings. Then you enhance that with the Encore machine and play it back through the phones again and so on, until you get lower brain music with red noise, the real shit. Only he said he thought I was good for this job. Me, who can't carry a tune. Just for laughs I said yes, and because sure I wanted to hear this murder, why not? So I put on the headphones and got ready to sing *The Saints Come Marching In.*

What I heard at first was too faint to make out, then I realized it was somebody humming, mumbling music—it was that old bum Mel Hankers singin *Walkin the Floor Over You.* I could hear the sound bouncin off that cast-iron building, for christ sake somebody really did kill the old fart just like I almost did. I hear the bottle break I could almost hear the killer's eyes as he bends over ready to cut the old bastard's throat. . . .

I pull off the headphones. I never killed him, I say.

Wally grins. Sure you did, Red, but it don't matter. The camera crew had a trick mike, they got sound and pictures of the whole thing. But who cares, I just want to borrow your neurons. Even a murderer has his uses.

The camera crew I figure will be easy to shut up, they only talked to the boss so far. I test the cord of the headphones, it's strong enough.

In Tibet, Wally says, they got a flute made out of the thighbone of a murderer, they know all about red noise, and they got these talking bowls, ever hear of them?

I say nothing I'm waiting for the fear to come up in his eyes but so far nothing, that's bad. I mean I gotta work myself up to murder by remembering things, that squashed frog twitching around, those pop festivals where somebody down in the crowd gets stabbed or torn up with chains or just kicked to death, old Mel with his hair hangin out of his nose as he tried to sing with his throat cut, marchin bands goin off to war with their dumb music pretendin there wasn't no poison gas barb wire no flame throwers no incendiary bombs no bombs full a steel darts no napalm no tanks throwin white phosphorus, no softnose bullets no machine guns no shrapnel no mines no rockets no nukes nothin but poop-de-poop music on a nice day, singers who fall dead with the needle hangin outa their arm who drown and crash and set fire to themselves and take too many pills and get shot by kids who think they love them. . . .

These talking bowls, he says, are made of some special alloy, they don't really talk but they do put out quite a train of sound. The Tibetans strike the bowl and hold it in both hands so the body of the musician becomes like the sounding board for the bowl. The tone starts out pure and simple (and here I realize Wally is afraid all right, he's just yakkin to keep me from moving) pure and simple but then it builds up all these resonances in funny waves until it begins to sound just like the cries of a thousand tortured souls in hell, if you listen you can hear each one, each kind of torment, of—

I get the cord around his neck, then he gets away for a second and he says, no listen what I wanted to say was computers are like castrati they don't know. Then I get the cord around his neck and shut him up for good. I only got a jack-knife so cuttin open his chest takes awhile but finally I get the heart out and put it in a shoebox, that only seems fair.

That's just about the whole story, I hadda get it all recorded before the cops get here, I hear the sirens now. Wally says at one time sirens was women who sat in this field of flowers singin. Only under the flowers the place was all full of piled up skeletons, some of em with gray meat hangin on, dried out gray meat.

Which I guess is all I will be when you play this back.

* * *

"Not as good as his last release, though."

"What do ya expect? Poor guy's been dead coupla hundred years, maybe he's gettin' tired. I mean how many times can they recycle him?"

"I liked the squashed frog okay. But the music wasn't up to the words this time. Slow stuff like that don't bleed me at all. I guess I like the modern better. Modern and live."

"Me too, hey, you goin to the big concert Saturday? It's Roger O'Hammerstein."

"With his ball-peen hammer, terrific! I heard he killed fourteen kids at his last concert. Fourteen!"

"Great! Not that I wanna get killed myself, exactly."

"No me neither."

"But maybe blinded would be okay."

"Sure, blindness I could handle, there's still music. But death—well, like. . . ."

"Like being in a second ending."

AFTERWORD

In 1981 I was asked to contribute to an anthology of science fiction stories concerned with music. My ignorance of music is profound, and I tend to be rather defensive about it. My thoughts therefore turned to defensiveness itself, and to offensiveness, and to the relation between music and violence.

I suppose the thesis is pretty obvious, if one thinks of the Nazis and Wagner, or the importance of music in Hitchcock films, or the Orpheus myth, or even British skinheads today with their combination dance/fights. The connection might be that music often helps repressed or inarticulate people express their emotions—the people who otherwise express them violently.

The Orpheus myth, I like to think, contains a certain kind of truth about music and violence. I like to think of it as a cautionary tale about what happens if you give yourself over to emotions entirely; you fall apart. Alas, like most Greek myths, the Orpheus story is also blindly anti-feminist. Evidently the Greeks, like a few modern sages (fewer all the time) thought that emotions were essentially feminine. Anyone who's seen a football game (songs again) knows better.

So let's all hear it, The Banks of the Ohio *or maybe* Hawaiian War Chant. . . .

Guesting

"At last, a real swift Moon," chumbles the general. He stands with his back to the room, staring out the great curved window. General Veet is not a well man; these past few days (weeks?) of interrogation have not been easy on any of us. The hands behind his back do not signal composure: the right desperately grasps the thumb of the left. If only he could cope like Nancy! But a relaxing chat with Jeb may yet help upgrade matters.

I am glad to occupy myself with this journal. Relief is mine in abling at last to set down some of my new experiences. All during the weeks (months?) of interrogation I was naturally denied access to any tools of fiction.

Such as television. It was through television that I first came to know these people, I feel sure. Long before I intruded in their planet's dust, I was privileged to watch them selling one another pizza-flavored taco-burgers, germicidal electronics and dog sugar. Soon I am to play a modest part in all this.

I cannot remember the crash itself. Was I buzzing a radar station, as sometimes they hint? I only know that I did crash, and that I must have been thrown clear of the saucer before its total annihilation by radar. As I learned later, my survival was truly miraculous: "On any other turkey farm," Veet said, "you'd be a dead letter."

This farm was owned by the breeder-inventor Snell McLube, now famous but unknown a year before when he'd launched his "self-stuffing" turkeys on the Thanksgiving market. Alarmed by his audacity, certain large Western sage cartels had tried tying him up in court with various nuisance suits, while they urged the FDA to initiate carcinogenic testing. With his money running out, McLube agreed to sell his patent to the cartel for suppression. In return, he demanded an exclusive nationwide franchise on sage pillows (the popular insomnia cure). A reluctant bargain was struck.

At the same time, McLube's ever-fertile imagination had moved on to "Sha-ho-fun", or rice vermicelli. He'd found a species of roundworm—a harmless parasite on his self-stuffers—that built itself termite-like tunnels of edible starch. By selective breeding, and by adding to the worm's diet his own artificial rice flavouring, McLube found he could produce instant Sha-ho-fun in any quantity, without rice.

He began stockpiling huge "haystacks" of the vermicelli, kept dry by many layers of plastic and surplus sage pillows, as he prepared for a main assault on the vast Chinese market. It was one of these haystacks that broke my fall. The sage may also have contributed to my amnesia.

I awoke to the acrid smell of glass and nylon. There were odd sensations of motion, mechanical noises, harsh human voices gargling away just as they do on television. I opened my eyes to a screen filled with flickering white. My translator was turned on, but not adjusted to deal with the flurry of idiom:

"... try to deal relationships, you know? In a very positive, human way ... finance needs enthusing ..."

"With me it was God, God, God, all the way."

"... were made out of brass, and when he clanged them together ..."

"... real swift moons ..."

"Kant always insisted that the physical things in space and time were real, see? Anybody who says Kant was an idealist is just fulla shit, man."

"... a Gettysburger with lettuce and ..."

I could turn my head, despite the ropes and clamps, and see a number of humans wearing shapeless blue bags over their heads. This had to be the military. When the one driving stopped us, the puzzling white streaks became simple dots of falling snow. There was snow on the ground, too. Two of the humans descended and built a small column of snow, which I recognized as a "snowman". When they had completed it and urinated on it, we proceeded.

General Veet continues to stare out the window at the darkness of parking lots. This world has so many parking lots, so many elevators, so many cafeterias. Even television could not prepare me for the dazzle.

At first there was only interrogation, which I suppose is the same anywhere: drugs, hypnosis, beatings, painful stuff, combined with offers of food, freedom, a high school diploma . . .

Q: Where is your home planet?

A: I really don't know.

Q: In this galaxy?

A: What's——?

Q: I'll ask the questions, space swine dog! Now just look at this star map and point to your home star.

A: Frankly one star looks pretty much like another to me. Sometimes I can pick out the Big Dipper the Plough the Wain Ursa Major the Great Bear. (Sometimes the translator shows off.)

Q: How does your spacecraft operate?

A: I'm no good with mechanical things. I imagine it has some kind of power or fuel or something and—ouch, don't.

And always in the dark there would be the sound of Veet's thumb cracking, cracking.

My amnesia seems total; with two exceptions we learned nothing about my previous life.

I did come up with one glimpse of myself flying along in my flying saucer. There is a potted begonia sitting on the instrument panel.

The other remembered fact is that I am skilled in hypnosurgery. Indeed, I am to demonstrate it tonight, by curing Nancy's pathological fear of seals. Phocophobia is not uncommon in military families, I find; several of the interrogation team have afflicted relatives. But I feel particular affection for Nancy Veet, as for her poor father.

This waiting room is large, fit for hundreds, but we three "tonight's guests" are its only occupants: General Beaujangles Veet, his daughter Nancy, and my true self. Only us on an ocean of orange carpet, waiting as we have waited all day for rehearsals, makeup calls, prop fittings. Television people do not, it seems, trust reality to happen only once. All must be arranged and rehearsed. Yet this Jeb Mason Show is watched by a thousand thousand thousand souls.

I have rehearsed many ways of making my entrance. An official named Lionel something—Wormcast, was it?—keeps changing everything. First he ordered me to appear wearing roller skates on my hands, and to present Jeb Mason with a silver doughnut. A joke had been written for Jeb to make.

But no, then I was to wire-fly across the stage, wearing a neon-light collar and carrying a mouthful of gold coins, which I was to spit into an upright tuba.

But no, now instead there will be a pink fur cage carried on by four men dressed as parrots; inside will be a washing machine filled with bananas. Under cover of a simulated explosion this will be whisked out of sight on a revolving stage which also brings into view Nancy pelting me with starfish while her father sings "The Umbrella Song". I'll wear a purple leopard skin; Nancy, copper lamé. The producers feel that this is sufficiently "alien" to tell the audience that something new is happening. I see nothing new in it.

I learned that my interrogation by the military was over, in the most offhand manner. I was in my cell at the base, where the base dentist (a trusted mute) was fitting me with dentures to replace teeth lost in questioning. General Veet came in wearing, not his usual drab uniform, but a casual suit of mustard yellow. The dentist, who was also blind, was unaware of this. He supposed my startled exclamation to be a groan of pain.

Without a word, Veet handed me a freshly decoded message:

As for our neighbour's family, there were
Attn relevant personnel: As of today, projects
seven of them and they were drawn
to be wound down include projects Alien
with seven oranges, a thing quite out
Soybeans to Zweiback Galore; excludable themes might
of taste, no variety in life, no
be nonfood color or piano scent. Color
composition in the world. We desired to
piercingly piano rushes through our celestial budget

have something done in a brighter style . . .
(mauve) towards ongoing "piano galore" be's
unmanageable . . .
My wife desired to be represented as
Thrawn Janet's celestial budget of puttylike attention
Venus, with a stomacher richly set with
grasps soybeans galore! Steamish Prussian Melba
soybeans?
diamonds, and her two little ones as
Goose down from budgies? Putty methods: attention!
Cupids by her side, while I, in
blinding reports from central office ignored! Piano.
my own gown and band, was to
crooked band DNA down own paradoxical budget
present her with my books on the Whistonian controversy.
gifts from soybeans. Crooked Bacon, blind, rushes
home cooking.

"A book code? But why use a long quotation from Goldsmith, if they only want to tell you to stop questioning me? It makes it all so unwieldy, like a kitchen painting that . . ." I tried to say, but the dentist clamped a rubber mask firmly over my face and I entered the poppy fields of sleep.

I feel sleepy now, and envy Nancy her industry. When we first arrived here in the orange-carpeted room, Nancy took from her bag a small coping saw and a disc of smooth elm plywood. She has spent her time creating a portrait, delicately-pierced, of J. Edgar Hoover. The name will be picked out in those delightful little brass nails she calls *flewets*. Nancy has I think learned great patience, being both an army daughter and seal-shy.

My patience is wearing, since Lionel Wormcast came by to change things again. Now I am simply to walk in, wearing an ordinary suit. The only extra will be a bathing cap (for my poor horns).

Veet's knuckle is popping like an outboard motor.

"The public has to be told, but gently," he said. "Press releases like these can ease the way a little." He showed me a sheaf of documents with headlines like FLYING SAUCERS COULD BE McCOY, EXPERTS AGREE; SPACE VISITORS FRIENDLY VEGETARIANS?; SPACE ALIENS 'JUST FOLKS'; and finally SPACEYS MAY SAVE WHALE. "But what we're really counting on is the Jeb Mason Show. Once people see you on Jeb Mason, they know you're real. They know you happen. Anything else is just uncontrollable rumor.

"Luckily there's a slot opening up early next year. That gives us time to get ready."

"Ready."

He cracked a knuckle. "You can't go on the goddamn Jeb Mason Show and say you got amnesia. We'll fake up some stuff for you: your planet's got a purple sky and three moons, you count with a duodecimal system, you fight dragons a lot, et cetera, et cetera. We'll get historians to write you a little history, physicists to figure out how your saucers fly, linguists to make up a language."

"But I'll never learn all that!"

"Just learn highlights and fake it. You'll only be talking for five minutes, tops. You throw in a phrase like 'Relief is mine in abling to be here tonight' and they'll eat it up."

"I could never talk like that," I protested. "Maybe I should do something instead of talk. I could do some hypnosurgery, maybe cure somebody of a phobia or something."

A knuckle shot its warning. "You leave Nancy alone," he said. It was the first I'd heard of Nancy.

The technique for curing any phobia is quite simple. The sufferer is made to imagine that he or she is a loose page in a dictionary read by his mother or her father. The name of the feared object is on that page, and becomes visible as the page slips out and begins fluttering towards the fire. A salad basket intervenes (the hypnotist) and, after a feigned erasure, administers an imaginary injection of reserpine. It remains only to wedge the sufferer's legs between two grand pianos and awaken him or her. I have never known this cure to fail. Yet I feel uneasy. I wish Beaujangles and Nancy had not agreed to this.

I studied highlights of alien behavior in any case, and I was given opportunities to show off in secret: lunch with the President, and a private audience with the Pope.

I can't say the Presidential lunch went badly, but it was curious. The President was seated at a large table among a dozen advisers. Though he saw me and nodded as I sat down, I do not think he knew who I was. All of his conversation seemed to be with Hal Gettysburger, his adviser on silver bullion.

The meal began with grapefruit, which I find poisonous; then green salad, which my assumed religion forbids; and finally turkey stuffed with rice vermicelli—to which I have an allergy. The President ate nothing, but drank plain water through the meal. His advisers all followed suit. As we all gave dessert a miss (tapioca, I'd heard, was derived from a poisonous root) the adviser next to me asked if I knew how tax shelters were erected on my planet. Before I could reply, the President rose and the meal was at an end.

I met the Pope at Castel Gandolfo, his summer residence: though it was January the air was summer-warm and clear enough to sit outdoors. His Holiness drowsed in a chair of Venetian glass. Its purple, red and green fire matched that of a few tiny brilliant creatures hovering about his shoulders: humming birds.

"They pick the wax from one's ears," he laughed, batting them away. "But they are a nuisance. Sit down, my child."

I took the plain glass chair opposite and waited. An hour or more of silence followed. I could not determine whether His Holiness was thinking, meditating or sleeping. Finally, as he got up to go, he said, "Immanuel."

"Immanuel," I murmured politely.

"Immanuel Velikovsky," came the impatient reply. "That's the name I was trying to think of. You have read his interesting theory no doubt? He says that Earth once cracked smack into Venus, killing all the dinosaurs."

"Indeed?"

"Yes, yes, and it also parted the Red Sea for Moses." I nodded.

"Read it, my child, read it." He prepared to give me his

blessing. "You above all should be conversant with these latest scientific findings."

Lionel drifts in to give us the final line-up tonight: Hand-jive star Bi Wredge, who was to have given the show a visual opening, has tennis elbow, so we lead off with pitcher Don Obergass of the Connecticut Yankees; followed by Siamese twin pianists Dewey and Sherm; then comes "Father" Jasper Tunxis, an ex-priest now doing religious market research. For a change of pace, impressionist Morm Zinger will then imitate articles of clothing, before eminent faith lawyer Duck Hubb chimes in with a more serious note. We're on last, in the "ordinary folks" slot.

Scarcely has Mr Wormcast finished filling us in when the great wall-screens in our orange-bottomed cage flicker into life. "It's the JEB MASON SHOW!" comes the hysterical announcement, above an insistent riff of trumpets. "And here he is—JEB THE MAN!"

The laconic pitcher Don Obergass opens the show badly, speaking briefly of a hobby, ant-crucifixion, before making way for the twins. Joined from head to pelvis along their common spine, they sit on one bench to two pianos, to play a few bars of Hahnemann's *Die Organon* before the commercial. Nancy drops her coping saw, and when she picks it up, I notice that her hand is trembling. The sight of two pianos? J. Edgar is beginning to look ragged, unkempt.

Father Tunxis describes a home computer, available to shut-ins, which is capable of saying 10^{14} rosaries a minute. I try to remember my duodecimal multiplication tables, my mind is a blur if that is possible, I can't remember the details of the saucer engine, something to do with piping the strangeness from quark to quark in a field of anti-nothingness? I watch the piles of sawdust beneath Nancy's chair deepen; the features of Hoover go from unkempt to leprous.

A commercial melody: hair sugar, cat soap, frozen charcoal are hawked before Duck Hubb appears:

"Well you see, Jeb, faith law is just another approach to law. We feel orthodox lawyers are all right as far as they go, but sometimes they don't really reach the client. They treat the client like a batch of paper, you know? The client's not a person, he or she is just a 'case', you know? This one is a divorce, maybe, and that one is a breach of contract, and over there is a libel. But people aren't just cases, they're human beings. We faith lawyers try to treat the whole client, yeah? Myself, I try to find out what the client really needs and wants. Instead of picking around in dusty lawbooks or manufacturing paperwork full of whereases and parties of the first part, I just sit down with my client and we ask God to look up the precedents for us. I put my hand on the client's head and try to *feel* where the trouble is. And do you know, ninety-nine times out of a hundred, *we go to court and we win! We win!* Because, you know, God is the real party of the first part, right?"

Tremendous applause cut off at its peak for a commercial. Lionel Wormcast comes into the lounge holding up his clipboard defensively. He's hardly able to look at us as he delivers the bad news:

"Look kids, I'm real sorry, but we had this last-minute change. See, we were negotiating with Leon Earl Poge, only there were all these loose ends. We weren't sure he'd be out of jail today, and the company that manages him wanted a little more money than we felt he was really worth—but I'm glad to say we made the deal five minutes ago. So you're bumped, real sorry. Of course we'll pencil you in for a slot later in the year. But speaking personally I guess you don't have much of a chance there either; things like an alien from space don't have a long shelf life . . . "

The face of J. Edgar Hoover was by this time entirely dissolved in elm sawdust. Nancy let the meaningless plywood ring fall to the carpet. "Oh I've made such a mess. I'll get something and clear it up," she says, sighing.

General Veet turns from the window at last. "Leon Earl Poge? You're dumping us for Leon Earl Poge? A four-star general, a genuine extraterrestrial alien from the other side of the galaxy or somewhere, and a big-production hypno-surgical cure—I don't believe this, you want to throw all that away for one lousy mass murderer? Goddamnit, Lionel, you can have a mass murderer anytime, anytime!"

Lionel nods in sympathetic circles. "Kids, if the decision was up to me . . . But this Poge is quite a character, you know? I mean, to murder twenty-eight people in a supermarket, and then to serve only one week of your sentence before they have to let you out on a technicality, you have to be qu-ite a char-act-er."

His indulgent chuckle goads Veet on to more undignified pleading. "What about this?" he cries, and strips off my bathing cap. The emissile horns, pressed flat for hours, shoot out to their full length. My headache eases. "He's got *antennae*, damnit, how's that for character?"

Lionel shrugs. "They look like snail horns to me. Kind of dumb and slow. I mean no disrespect to your geek here, but why don't he go to a good plastic surgeon and have them cut off? They're no good to us, we ain't running a freak show, kids."

On the giant screens, Leon Earl Poge was still an insignificant figure in a brimless hat. "I'm sorry I done it," he was saying. "But yeah, I guess I would do it again."

"Where's Nancy?" I said, suddenly alarmed.

For some time I haven't abling to make any more entries in this journal. My life seems to have gone adrift. Everything flowed so fast through the Bernoulli tube of the Jeb Mason Show, but slower before and after. Now I lack either the viscosity to take hold of life as I find it or the pressure to push on past to something new. My life-flow is at times laminar, at times turbulent, with occasional cavitations like the death of Nancy.

General Veet blames me for everything, naturally: His career is in tatters, we did not get on the Jeb Mason Show, his daughter is dead and finally he has just learned he has a tumor of the left thumb. Yet tragedy has strangely brought us closer together, even if he does plan to kill me.

I recently had my horns removed by a Minneapolis cosmetic surgeon who chattered all through the operation about his favourite cartoon characters, a lion that does comic belches and others. In the waiting room I ran into Don Obergass, there to have a few more sweat-glands removed from an already dry and deadly pitching palm. Afterwards we took a captive balloon to the overhead shopping mall and exchanged news. Don toyed with the idea of giving up pitching to devote more time to ant-crucifixion.

"It's a painless process, you know? The ants really enjoy it."

"Come on babe, that's what fox-killers say about their prey."

"True though . . . how can I explain? One day in the dugout I was watching this anthill. And I noticed how much like a miniature Passion Play it all looked, you know? The orderly processions, the sense of something large and important taking place. . . ."

My anaesthetic had evidently not worn off: I kept dozing as we ascended.

"Getting the little buggers to carry a cross was the easy part. Call me crazy but I've always seen . . . pitcher as . . . st-fig . . . mound as Calvary? The cleats become nails, the rosin bag is vinegar and gall, the ball a pierced . . . where on the cap it says I.N. . . . the umpire a centurion, runners on first and third are the good thieves, you with me so far? Judas is up with two out in the bottom half of the ninth, no score and the crowd . . ."

"Wants Barabbas, he's in the bullpen," I interjected.

"Oh don't be stupid. Weren't you listening?"

I explained that I had a lot on my mind, and described the death of Nancy. The climax of our televised cure would have been a demonstration that Nancy's phocophobia was indeed gone. For this purpose, a live seal in a tank had been brought into the studio. While searching for a broom to sweep up her elm sawdust, Nancy had blundered into the wrong room, to face the most feared object in the universe.

"Which turned out not to be you, poor thing," said Don. "Have you thought of trying ant-crucifixion?"

I said I couldn't help wondering why Don, a beautiful and intelligent woman and a successful ballplayer, indulged in this strange and destructive hobby.

She laughed. "That's what Morm says."

"Morm?"

"Morm Zinger, my husband. We met on the Jeb Mason Show—remember his impersonation of a broken tennis shoe?—and he calls me crazy! And here he is now, hi Morm."

The impressionist was just emerging from an elm store with a number of plywood discs under his arm. "Just something to take my mind off my researches," he apologized. It turns out that Zinger is tracing references in modern literature to brand names of clothing.

"There's a peculiar pattern emerging. For instance in *Ulysses*, at the funeral a man in a mackintosh turns up. No one knows him, and by mistake his name gets into the paper as M'Intosh. A man in the crowd.

"And again in *The Waste Land*, again in the burial part, another man in the crowd, someone knows him as 'Stetson'."

"Burial, man in crowd, clothing label," I said. "But where does it get us?"

"I'm not sure. It's as though a fully-clothed figure of mystery is trying to emerge through modern Western literature. Maybe these are mystical references to a new Messiah. I am still trying to run down a few promising leads, references to Levis, Hush Puppies and *The Bishop's Jaegers*." His manner is urgent, as though he believes I have some answer.

Don says, "Darling, did you remember the little elm crosses?" There is urgency in her tone too, and in the sound behind me of a gun being cocked or maybe a thumb knuckle being cracked.

AFTERWORD

Being an American living in England for so long that you feel un-American but not really English, is a reasonable preparation for thinking about aliens. It makes me a lot more interested in how aliens might feel about us than how they might look or act. In both this story and in "The Next Dwarf", I leave out physical details of the critturs.

The simple thesis of "Guesting", that not even a visitor from across the galaxy could hold a video audience for long, is borne out by the fact that no one can remember the great video sensations of only a year ago. I can't remember them either. Watching TV, we swim in a sea of high excitement, as our attention is directed now to a mass poisoner, now to a human fly, now to a nuclear power station going up in smoke, now to a little war in some small, distant country—to mention only news items.

I've just seen a clip from some American show on which a couple are invited to tell their problems to a ventriloquist and his dummy. But that's not all. They are then given advice by a psychologist, a minister and an astrologer. But that's not all. The studio audience then press buttons to vote for the best advice, and the couple also make their choice. If they agree with the audience, they win some money. If this program is a success, one can imagine expanded versions adding advice from Texas prostitutes and Mafia hit men, oil sheiks and, what the heck, comic book superheroes. Maybe even aliens.

Absent Friends

When it was the robot's turn to tell a story, it first raised its glass in a toast.

"Absent friends."

The rest of us drank, while the robot held its empty glass to its painted smile. I don't know what the others thought of this gesture, but it made me uneasy, as always. I've been travelling to Mars and back for over fifteen years—Eagleburg and Eurograd being my sales territory for Hogpress Sportswear—so I've been in a lot of taverns like this one, where travellers sit around the fake fire and swap fake stories. But every time I see a robot taking a fake drink from an empty glass, I feel uneasy. The world seems all wrong, you know?

"Absent friends," the robot said again. "Some more absent than others." The painted smile never wavered. "Sitting here with all of you around this fire reminds me of some absent friends of mine, people I sat around another fire with, swapping stories, a long time ago. Back in '32 it was, when I shipped out for Mars in a tub called the *Migraine*."

"As a steward?" someone asked.

"Certainly not! The *Migraine* was a union ship—no robot work allowed, or the whole fleet would have walked out. No, I was a passenger on that accursèd vessel."

Someone asked, "Why accursèd?" The rest of us settled back, staring into the fire at the faces of our own absent friends or otherwise blanking our minds, ready for the tinhead's tale.

* * *

Call me Rusty (it began). I was on my way to Mars to help with some mission work in Eagleburg—the Reverend Orlando Mule Crusade, ever hear of it? Very big in those days. People liked Reverend Mule's way of preaching. He was a ventriloquist, see, and I guess that little dummy of his, Holy Rollo, was just about the most popular personality on Earth. Or on Mars. Reverend Mule was, I guess, a pioneer in ventriloquist preaching. He and his dummy used to turn up on TV every Sunday, along with the full company: the Orlando singers and dancers, the Mule choir, and so on. There was saturation broadcasting of the services by satellite to all parts of both planets.

I was sent to Mars to fill in for somebody, since I understudied all parts of the service. I could preach, heal, sing, everything. This time I had to play a hopeless cripple who gets an instant Crusade cure. The regular guy had slipped a disc throwing away his crutches.

The *Migraine* was not a happy ship. It was a freighter carrying mainly dairy cattle, but you could tell it hadn't always been so low-brow. I had a lot of time to wander about, and I found a few indications of former glory. There was the remains of a grand ballroom, its dusty gilt chairs piled in the corners, an eighty-meter cobweb running from the chandelier to a far corner where I found a faded dance card. There was a Gentlemen's Cloakroom with marble walls and sinks, two barber chairs and a shoeshine stand. There was a "First Class Only" coffee room where brocaded sofas rotted near the collapsed carcase of a grand piano. There, in the back of the drawer of a rosewood writing desk, I found a supply of notepaper with the curious heading, "SS *Van Dine*". Wasn't that the name of a ship that had vanished mysteriously, while crossing the notorious Bermuda Tetrahedron? I wasn't sure.

There was also an incomparable library where I spent long weeks and short months reading, viewing and listening. There was no one fixed pattern to my reading. For a time I chose only books in which robots named Robbie appeared; then I read only the autobiographies of ex-nuns.

It all helped take my mind off the constant problems aboard the *Migraine*. We seemed to hit more than our share of asteroid storms, first of all. Once a high-speed object which smashed its way through the hull and fifteen bulkheads before coming to rest, turned out to be a frozen Long Island duckling. How it came to be whizzing around in space was never explained, and it was just one more incident to make the crew uneasy.

The crew were Finns, so I was never able to find out what their quarrel was with the captain. He, the only English speaker, kept denying to me that there was any trouble aboard. But the men and women of the crew continued to gather in muttering groups, glower at the captain, and even brandish weapons. One day a mob of them appeared, holding aloft a spacesuit and marching towards the captain's cabin. I deduced that they intended to cast him adrift or perhaps maroon him on Deimos. But this mutiny was cut short by the next calamity: We were attacked by pirates.

I heard the captain's voice over the P.A.: "Pirates! We're being boarded!" Then a shot, a moment of silence, and then confused noises like figs being gulped rapidly by a dozen small dogs.

I kept out of the way, hearing shots from various parts of the ship, as the pirates killed off the entire crew. I relaxed and watched movies—the library had the excellent Russian version of *Finnegans Wake*—while I awaited further developments.

In the end, it didn't turn out too badly. Though the pirates wiped out all human life aboard, they spared me to cook and clean. Unfortunately, my cleaning was a little too energetic. One day I managed to knock the vacuum cleaner into some steering mechanism and break it. The good ship *Migraine* turned and headed straight for the sun.

At first, the pirate band were naturally upset to find out that we were soon to be "exalted" (as the astrologers used to say). But you can get used to anything. We decided not to spend our last days moping or complaining, but to make the best of them. To acclimatize everyone to the inevitable rise in temperature, we turned up the heat in advance. Food rationing began at once—not because there was any shortage, but to focus human minds on the ordeal ahead.

Since heat and starvation soon made most of the pirates insomniacs, we spent our time telling stories. These shared experiences bound us together closely, in a comradeship that had no regard for race, creed, color, sex, age, height, weight, IQ, identifying scars or even lack of protoplasm. We might be doomed or damned, but we were darned glad of the company.

Eventually the heat was so intense that the humans preferred not to touch the metal deck at all. They lay in hammocks while I brought them iced salt water. All groaned or gasped their way through their stories until it was the turn of one who claimed to be a former tree surgeon.

"It wasn't my only profession before piracy," he said. "Once I was a nuclear physicist."

Others expressed surprise.

"I've never bragged about it," he said, "because that's the kind of guy I am. I studied at Idaho Agricultural and Military College, which I admit is not a place famous for its contributions to pure science. Idaho A & M tended to concentrate on potato-related courses like the Biology of Potato Blight, Potato Printing Technology, and Spud Dietetics.

"But it so happened that my tutor was the brilliant eccentric but original Tang Wee. Professor Wee, in case anyone here doesn't know it, is the discoverer of 'absent particles'. These were predicted way back in 1951 by Luftworp, who, as you know——"

Our blank looks told him we didn't know. He explained:

"Luftworp was another loner. His work wasn't taken seriously until the turn of the century, partly because he had no formal academic credentials—he was a circus roustabout by trade—and partly because of the way he presented his papers. Despite being barely literate, Luftworp chose to put all of his work into verse. I remember one terrible sonnet:

> "When a right-hand, red, down quark emits
> A roseate *X* particle with charge
> Electric minus four-thirds, not too large,
> The dexter scarlet quark then loses its
> Name: A right-hand positron exits.
> Anon *X* particle of ruby hue doth barge
> Into a green left-handed up quark, marg-
> Inally southpaw verdure changing: It's
> Metamorphosed to an antiblue
> Left-handed anti- (up) quark, so it seems . . . "

One of the other pirates signalled that the recitation was over by drawing his gun and smiling oddly. The physicist smiled too, saying, "I forget the rest. Anyway, the endings of his poems were never important. In fact, his greatest work, *On the Orangeness of Absence*, has only one line. I puzzled over it for years before I met Luftworp in person—he was a very old man then, on his third heart and second liver—and I asked him outright.

" 'Sir, is one line enough to express one of the fundamental truths upon which is built the entire edifice of modern physics?'

"He sat for a long moment, turning the champagne glass in his gnarled hand. Did I mention we were at a banquet in his honor? And even though he was no longer allowed to eat or drink anything, they'd put an empty glass into his hand. He sat turning it for a moment, then he said, 'Okay, smartass, you find a rhyme for "orange" and I'll write another line.' My opinion of Luftworp's work was lowered from that moment.

"Others, however, regard his work as classical. He did after all lay the theoretical foundations for *absent particles*, by showing that absence and antiabsence are essential properties like charm or spin or——"

At this point, several of the other pirates interrupted to complain they didn't know what he was talking about. He responded with a long lecture on hadrons, leptons, mesons, three kinds of neutrino, five kinds of quark, eight gluons, antiparticles and so on. He then went on to list all the properties these particles could possess. We all followed him as he explained that particles could have different masses and charges, even different energies and spins. But we were lost when he moved on to more mysterious properties like color, charm and strangeness. "It's very simple," he kept saying. "A quark comes in red, green or blue, and for each color there are six theoretical flavors. . . ."

That, he emphasized, was only the beginning. "In the 1960s two researchers called Disch and Sladek found a particle called the Nullitron which changed everything. The Nullitron has no properties of any kind, and is in fact not very interesting. But its existence (or not) opened up new possibilities. Before long, others were finding particles with many new properties: odor, feel, political persuasion, average attendance and gas mileage. Then Tang Wee, following Luftworp, found the most significant property of all: *absence*.

"I remember well the day when Nobel prizewinner Giro Poloni sent his famous telegram to Wee congratulating him on his discovery: 'Absence will make the art go yonder'. That's just what happened, too. Theoretical work became even more metaphysical than ever, and research followed. I myself studied bubble chamber photos to see what did not appear on them ... confirmed Wee's conjecture that ... gravity due to ... objects being pushed together by the pressure of absent. . . ."

I found myself dozing—the heat was intense and my batteries were low—as the pirate physicist launched into an incomprehensible lecture on his own work: "... breadstick model ... not unscalar ... identical with the particles they replaced. ... Quirks, digamma mesons, the lumps on nutria ... sex, said the travelling ... scampi divided against itself cannot. ... Huron! Yet when ... neoclassical angle, guys and gals, so. ... Weeons by contrast do not ... go gently ... gluons may predominate, but strapons lend elegance ... the rest is history, into that ... goodnight.

"Well, Wee himself was a Nobel winner, and so it was he who sent me the enigmatic telegram, 'Weep articles no win absent Iago's nap'. I think it was really meant to read 'Wee particles now in absentia go snap', but who knows for sure? These Nobel winners always try to squeeze in under ten words, so they end up with gibberish. Any questions?"

Someone asked about the Manhattan project.

"Doomed from the start. Couldn't have been worse if they'd actually held it in Manhattan—or spent their time on a new manhattan recipe. Of course with America at war, they couldn't admit their failure. So instead of backing down, they claimed to be working next on a bigger and better project, a superbomb. Then of course Russia had to make the same claim, and by then the lie was so big everybody had to keep it going.

"Everyone went right on supposedly testing bombs

equivalent to megatons of TNT. If you check the records carefully, however, you'll see there are megatons of *real* TNT not accounted for!"

I spoke up. "Wait just a minute. Are you trying to tell us it's all a fraud? That there are no atomic bombs? No hydrogen bombs? No tactical nukes, nothing?"

"Correct. You see, there can't be repeated tests of a genuine nuclear weapon. Because the first time you set it off, an anti-chain anti-reaction would ripple through all the absent anti-particles of the universe—blowing everything to kingdom come."

"Yeah? Then what about nuclear power stations?"

"I was just getting to those," he said. "All part of the world fraud. Those who maintain it argue that we've had three-quarters of a century of relatively peaceful times, just because everybody was afraid of 'the Bomb'. But it's incredibly complicated. Nuclear power stations all have to be built right on top of coal seams or near oil pipelines. The military has to pretend to stockpile all those imaginary weapons. Notice that nobody ever gets to see these stockpiles? No, and I'll tell you why. Soon as anybody gets a peek at a real 100 megaton bomb, the game is up. Because there it is, one huge ball of TNT, over 300 meters in diameter, weighing a hundred million tons—and of course no missile or plane ever made could deliver it as a weapon."

One of the other pirates spoke up. "Kind of hard to believe all this, my son. I mean, why should all the scientists and all the governments of the world be lying to us and you alone telling us the truth? You got any proof?"

The physicist nodded and held out his fist. "The proof is right here. This, ladies and gentlemen, is an absent semi-anti-nullitron." He opened his fist to reveal a red wooden ball about an inch in diameter. "I know it may seem a trifle big for a subatomic particle, but that can't be helped. The fact is, this little mother is going with us to the sun. And when it hits the sun, *pow*! The whole universe is going to burn up with us!"

The ball fell from his sweaty grasp and rolled away under some lockers. While he got down to look for it, the rest of us avoided each others' gaze. The least giggle could set off a chain reaction.

I couldn't help saying, "Some proof. Listen, this ship is nuclear-powered. It's not powered by enormous dynamite explosions or by some nearby coal mine, dammit. We're in space, headed for the sun. Even you have to admit that. Your little red bead can't blow up the sun otherwise, right?"

But when he brought the bead out, it was green. "I guess you're right, Rusty," he said. "I guess I'm in the middle of some fundamental paradox here that——"

So saying, he and the bead popped out of existence.

One of the other pirates said, "I guess he was wrong about the fundamental nature of *—oops!*" He too vanished.

Another pirate said, "We all have to be careful, not to think too much about this, don't you see? Because either the universe contains him and all his funny particles and ideas and *no* nukes, or else it contains the absence of a green wooden——"

One by one they succumbed, unable to resist the temptation to analyse. The penultimate pirate almost had the answer as she vanished, saying: "It's almost a trap for critics, each critical analysis becoming part of the analysed story*—aha!*"

The last pirate, a tall, stooped man with a lugubrious expression accentuated by the heavy moustache that he kept dyed green, was Boru Puxj, former attaché at the Chilean Embassy on Mars, until recalled for various offences, the least of which was impersonating an orthodontist. But why do I tell you all this? No doubt to put off for as long as possible the moment of his death; for he, too, succumbed to fatal reason.

"I've got to find out!" he cried, and, seizing a fire-axe, he attacked the hull of the ship itself. Since the hull was made mainly of thin canvas, stretched over a wooden frame and painted, he had no trouble ripping a large hole in it. Through the hole at once rushed the ship's air, the fire-axe and Boru Puxj.

I held on to a convenient stanchion and peered out into black space. Against the gleaming dust of stars, I could make out his sunlit figure spinning, spinning. And as it blinked out of sight, the space scene was instantly replaced by a peaceful Earthly landscape. I saw a hillside, clouds above trees, and in the middle of it all a large coal mine. Conveyors were carrying a continuous stream of coal to the ship's engines. I never asked why.

I alone am left to tell this tale.

* * *

"I don't want to be smug," the robot finished, "but I think the reason I did survive is because I never questioned or analysed anything—*oops!*" With a terrible clang, it was dragged out of our universe.

One of the others said, "Wait a minute, was this a coffin ship, or what? I mean, isn't it just possible that the owners tried to scuttle her in space to collect the insurance?" *Wham.*

"That's not it," said another. "Remember he found all that stationery marked SS *Van Dine*? Well, wasn't this *Van Dine* that mysterious space freighter they found drifting in space—not a soul on board but with the dinner still on the table? Well then——" *Wham.*

"I've only got one question: how about those hammocks? People lying around in hammocks in a free-falling space ship? Unless maybe it was on Earth all along——" *Zip.*

"Must be an allegory about modern anomie or——" *Pop.*

"Will everybody please just stop analysing here? Because we too are inside it, and unless we're very, very careful, we might all—*ow!*"

One by one they go, until I am left alone by the fake fire. But my glass is empty and my smile feels fixed, and now that I think of it, is that fire fake? It blazes like the sun, which we now know is built near a very large, very efficient coal mine, right? So if you'll all raise your glasses, the toast is——

AFTERWORD

This began life as a tiny section in my novel, Tik-Tok, *a piece of padding that didn't work. I had always wanted to write a novel which, like the Thousand and One Nights, includes stories within stories within stories. I may yet write such a novel, but it'll have to be planned. In this case, a straight narrative suddenly veers off into a few apparently pointless stories. Friends persuaded me to cut it, and I haven't regretted their advice.*

I include it here because I still think it's funny, and because it continues my fake science articles. The ways of subatomic physics are not my ways, I guess. While I can puzzle my way through an article on the subject in Scientific American, *I know at the end that my understanding is tenuous. In a day or so I'll once more forget the difference between a baryon and a hadron (if there is a difference). This may sound as though I'm bragging about my ignorance, but not so. I really would like to understand at least one tiny bit of physics—maybe just one quark.*

After Flaubert

Mr Bosch and Mr Jones sat waiting to tee off. The weather, unseasonably hot for this part of Ireland, made them take off the caps they'd bought especially for this holiday and put them beside them on the bench. Jerry Bosch looked into Jones's rustic Irish-style cap and read HONG KONG. Ford Jones looked into Bosch's modified tam and read JAPAN. They caught one another looking, laughed, and slipped easily into a discussion of Orientals: treacherous on the whole, though one had to admire the Japs' business savvy.

Bosch's company made crisps; Jones's specialized in toiletries; they were surprised at how much they had in common. Both had promised their wives this holiday; both wives were off visiting the same ruined abbey; both husbands found the Irish altogether too glib, the French devious, and their own countrymen lacking in backbone. The British economy—a disaster. The drought—a tragedy.

"I understand it's the CIA behind it," said Bosch. "They've been mucking about with weather control, trying to ruin the Russian wheat harvest. The floods in Russia, you see, have taken all our rain."

"Really? I thought it seemed unnatural, the Thames drying up and all. But the wife read somewhere that it was all to do with sunspots."

"Women get the strangest ideas! *My* wife says it's all part of the great collapse of everything. Written up in Nostradamus, so she says."

They chuckled over the folly of women, especially in politics. What was really needed, they resolved, was some sort of men's liberation movement. As for Women's Lib, wasn't it just a diversion, taking everyone's mind off the real issues?

"You've put your finger on it, Bosch. We've been decimalized and metricated to death, taxed into starvation, and beaten to our knees by the bloody oil sheiks."

"Even Iceland doesn't respect the Royal Navy any more. Britain is becoming an international joke."

"There you have it! We've lost respect for ourselves. We let the trades union militants hold the country to ransom; the pound starts its long, slow downward slide; and the next thing you know the country's full of immigrants on the dole, grabbing all the color TVs and new cars they can get. It's *cause and effect.* And no one gives a damn about the pensioners."

Bosch agreed. That evening, when the two couples dined together, he started to talk about anarchy, and the need for a return to the spirit of the Blitz.

Elizabeth Bosch said, "Jerry, I hope we're not going to talk politics all evening. We're on holiday, for heaven's sake! I don't want *my* digestion ruined."

"Stress kills," said Jones amiably.

"But so does this, darling." Norma Jones held up a bite of pink Westport ham. "*Cholesterol.* The number-one cause of heart disease."

Elizabeth begged to differ. Cholesterol was said to cure cancer. She'd read as much in the same place where she'd read that beans cause blood clots. The safest thing was to stick to honey, yoghurt, and all brown foods. "You see, white bread is just so much sawdust, and white eggs are anaemic, and white sugar—well, it's *lethal.*"

"But honey must have sugar in it," Bosch objected. "It's sweet."

"Not really," said Elizabeth. "You see, it's organic. Like say grapefruit."

"I tried a grapefruit diet a few years ago," said Norma. "But it made me dizzy. I found I was taking in too much Vitamin C. Maybe it wasn't organically grown, though."

Ford Maddox Jones said, "Norma, I keep trying to tell you, Vitamin C is *good.* Haven't had a cold since I started taking it, and you know it."

"You never did have colds. Vitamin C is deadly. Really, the best thing is one hundred per cent whole-grain cereals and very little liquid. It cures almost anything. Cancer, heart disease, and—they say it cured some of the victims of Hiroshima!"

Bosch laughed. "What do you mean, cured them? They were fried——"

"Cured them of radiation poisoning. I don't know exactly where I read it, but it's true."

"Well, maybe. One thing's sure. Most of the food you get nowadays is absolutely stuffed with poisons. They jab chickens with penicillin to make them tender or something. And have you ever read the list of ingredients on a tin of beans? Frightening."

"But everything's poisonous," said Jones. "Even common table salt is made up of two deadly poisons, you know."

"But not sea-salt," said his wife. She and Mrs Bosch turned to a discussion of organic and natural makeup: skin food made from almonds, slippery elm soap, placenta cream, avocado cream, green lettuce soap, egg wrinkle cream, egg membranes placed on the eyelids, elbows dipped in grapefruit halves, herbal shampoo, banana cream, wheat germ shampoo. Elizabeth believed that all makeup was bad for the skin, and that it was better to rely on pure soap and water. Soap, Norma informed her, was fatal to the complexion, drying out natural oils. But makeup could be beneficial, keeping the oils from leaking out.

Oil reminded Bosch of a rumor that St Paul's was being secretly purchased by certain Middle Eastern interests, to be turned into a mosque. Jones wondered whether the Arabs really considered sheeps' eyes such a great delicacy, after all.

". . . loganberry cream, rubbed on each night," said Elizabeth. "I understand she lived to the age of 86, without a single wrinkle."

Norma nodded. "Of course you know the main cause of all skin complaints: constipation. There's really nothing like colonic irrigation for clearing the skin. Oh, and the eyes. My aunt stopped wearing glasses, after she tried eye exercises and colonic irrigation."

"Sounds like agriculture in the Colonies," said her husband. "I prefer to call it lavage."

". . . and calling the faithful to prayer from the Post Office tower," Bosch concluded. He'd been drinking more than the others, and had missed a turn in the conversation. "What were you saying about exercising sheep's eyes?"

Jones put him straight. "But I'll tell you one thing, these Paki restaurants make curry for only one reason—to cover the taste of *cat*."

Elizabeth Bosch was upset. "Surely not! Surely the RSPCA wouldn't allow it!"

"Little do you know," said Norma. "They allow all sorts of horrid animal experiments all the time. Millions of pets snatched off to the laboratories, to be slowly cut to pieces while they make tape recordings of their screams! Ford, ask for the menu, will you? I think I'd like a sweet."

Over coffee the conversation turned to medical matters: wearing glasses caused cancer; contact lenses were worse. The new soft lenses—it was said that they had a nasty way of rolling back into the head and becoming lodged in the optic nerve. Bad vision was all in the mind anyway, or caused by maladjustments of the spine. Norma's aunt swore by chiropractors. There was something to be said for faith healing, too, even if it was only a kind of hypnosis. Jerry was building an orgone box, when he got round to it. Had anyone seen those fascinating TV films on acupuncture in China? Everyone had.

Norma said, "I think Nature knows best. There's a natural cure for every ailment known, if only we knew where to look for it."

"She's right, you know." Ford stirred brown sugar into his coffee. "The animals chew certain leaves and things when they're ill. And what about primitive people? Those South American Indians who found quinine. It's only because we've lost touch with Nature that we have all these big drug companies with their laboratories . . ."

". . . animal experiments . . ."

". . . and then they come up with something like Thalidomide! Or birth pills that give you blood diseases, is it?"

"Yes, or anabolic steroids, so these bloody Russian women can win gold medals all over the place . . . "

". . . snatch the heart and kidneys out of you before you even stop breathing . . . "

"Homeopathy? I don't know exactly, but the Queen Mother swears by it. Of course they can afford it, whatever . . ."

". . . all in the mind, anyway. They say if you put your mind to it, you can change your pulse rate and stop a heart attack in its tracks."

"I've heard that, too. They say you can do anything. Cure a third-degree burn, or is it first-degree? You can even grow new teeth!"

"Amazing, the human mind."

That subject led them, over brandy, then whisky, on to the psychic.

"Do you know," said Norma, "my aunt swears that when Uri Geller was on TV, her clock stopped?"

"Probably run down," said Bosch, whose amazing mind ran to scepticism. "She forgot to wind it?"

"She'd just wound it, an hour or so before. And it had never, ever stopped in all the years she'd had it. What do you say to that?"

Bosch shrugged. "Cases like that I'm not so sure about. But it could be some kind of radiation. Ever notice how you can stare at the back of someone's neck and make them turn round and look at you?"

All of them had noticed this effect. Ford Jones shook his head. "Radiation, eh? Is that what they say?"

"The scientists have pretty well proved it, by now. ESP, telepathy, whatever you want to call it—they've got it taped."

"On tape?" said Norma.

"Just an expression, I mean they understand it. Science has proved it exists. But wait, you've reminded me of something—now what was it?"

"I don't think science understands a damn thing," said Elizabeth. "Especially when it comes to occult matters. The scientists are just jealous because they can't do it as well. Predict things, and so on." She turned to Ford Jones. "What's your sign? No, wait, don't tell me. You're—must be—Aries?"

He shook his head. "Leo."

"I knew it was a fire sign. I very seldom miss."

"Are you an astrologer?"

She laughed. "No, I just dabble. But there's something in it, you know. Look at this year—all the earthquakes in Italy, drought in Britain, floods in Russia, economic crises—it must be the planets' conjunctions and things, mustn't it?"

Norma explained that the end of the world was coming in 1999, according to Nostradamus. Oh, the others might laugh (they did so), but Nostradamus was right about so many other things, like the world wars and Napoleon and Hitler—could we really afford to scoff at things we didn't understand?

"Nothing magical about it," Bosch insisted. "Nostradamus was just a scientist. Only science has forgotten all the old methods, like alchemy and so on. I think they'll be going back to the old ways soon. Stands to reason. I mean, the Egyptians didn't build a thing like the Great Pyramid for the hell of it, did they? Six billion or is it million tons of stone, all fitted together like the parts of a watch. But that reminds me——"

"I heard they took an X-ray of the Pyramid," said Jones. "But they wouldn't say what they saw inside it. They hushed it up." He began to ramble on about all the inventions science was always hushing up, such as a car that runs on water (oil sheiks bought up the patent) and a razor blade that never wears out.

"Funny you should say that," said Bosch. "They claim—the scientists claim—that if you make a little pyramid out of cardboard, and put a used razor blade under it overnight, it'll be sharp again in the morning."

Elizabeth found that hard to believe. Jones explained it to her in terms of radiation.

"But I remembered what I was going to say," said Bosch. "Stones. And tapes."

Elizabeth asked, "What's that supposed to mean? Jerry, are——?"

"No, listen. It's a new theory about *ghosts*."

Ford thought ghosts were a lot of hokum. Norma had been to a séance, however.

"The theory is ghosts are just images. The original images got embedded in the stones of, say, an old house, you see? Like on a video tape recorder. And then someone comes along with the right wave-length or whatever—someone psychic—and the tapes play for them."

"Ghosts," said Ford. "I think we all must be tired. You mean——?"

"Sure, take this old place, for instance. It used to be a castle, before they made it into a hotel. The stones here could be packed with images. Words, too. The right person could sit down here and call up every old—whoever it was—that ever lived here?"

"They could call us up, too," said Elizabeth. "In the future, say a hundred years, someone could see us and hear every word we said!"

Ford nudged her. "Don't say anything I wouldn't say!"

"But we'd be dead!"

They finished the evening by listing all the people they could name who were mysteriously dead: John Kennedy, Marilyn Monroe, Glenn Miller, Martin Bormann. . . .

AFTERWORD

It isn't enough to call Emma Tennant's Bananas *a magazine. Special quotation marks should be invented to mark its brilliance: The *magazine** Bananas. *It was one of the bright spots in Britain's slow slump into darkness during the 1970s, and it broke with all "little magazine" traditions. It published lots of fiction (almost no one else in Britain was publishing any). It was well-illustrated. It published the work of leading poets without ever being a stuffy establishment magazine. And just to make sure it was never taken too seriously,* Bananas *was printed as a tabloid newspaper and sold everywhere.*

Emma paid contributors (another innovation among little magazines). Moreover, Bananas *made a profit. It did not die of starvation, the usual little mag fate. Emma, needing more for her own writing, finally sold it to someone with different editorial ideas.* Bananas *was then no longer a *magazine*, only a magazine.*

Each issue had a "supplement" devoted to some theme, serious or silly. In one issue the supplement covered received ideas, or "Fac's". Having just read Flaubert's Bouvard and Pecuchet, *I couldn't help trying to catch some of its spirit for the above story. I don't know of anyone besides Flaubert, and occasionally Mark Twain, who made a careful study of the fac'-worshipping mind.*

The Brass Monkey

Pavel Roskan stood before the large window in Director's anteroom, trying to see his own reflection. He could not; not a ghost of his white hair and expensive tailoring moved among the shadows of pigeons flapping up in alarm or sailing down to settle on the ledge and grunt at one another. Pigeons disgusted Roskan. It was hard to believe that the late Dr Skinner had based so much of his work on the study of these filthy, grunting creatures. And of course these Westerners had practically canonized Dr Skinner, whose name, if Roskan translated it correctly, meant "he who flays". Still, one had to admire results. Roskan was only here, in fact, to admire some quite remarkable results.

He looked finally beyond the ledge down into the park, into a railed area where a few "soap-box" orators were trying to enrage a crowd. Almost no one seemed to be stopping or listening at all—no one except the "clowns". Odd way to handle a mob, he thought. The clowns did nothing, merely stood lounging here and there along the railing. But Roskan noticed how their painted faces scanned the crowd. As head of the police in his own country, he recognized them for men on duty. Very odd.

"Mr Roskan? Sorry to have kept you waiting."

He turned from the window. Director, a younger man than he'd expected, did not shake hands. "I was watching your plainclothesmen at the, er, Freedom Rally. But aren't their disguises——?"

Director flashed his boyish grin. "Not disguises, Mr Roskan. Those are the official uniforms of our crowd-control men. Everyone down there knows perfectly well who they are. Open government, you might say—though of course that's only part of the story."

He guided Roskan into his small, informal office. "You must think they look ridiculous, and of course that's the idea. Sherry?"

"But they—no thank you, alcohol I don't—but they *are*

ridiculous. How can people have respect for policeman with silly face? With nose like red pong-ping ball?" As usual, getting rattled made Roskan's English slip.

Director grinned again. "We want them to respect the law, not some bully in a uniform. After all, Hitler and his cronies took uniform-respect about as far as anyone could, didn't they? And with limited success. No, our aims are quite different, as you'll see. We hope ultimately to do away with policemen altogether. Let everyone be his own policeman."

Roskan tried not to show his contempt. "You surely do not believe you can stop people committing crimes?"

"Why not? You'll be surprised to find out how far we've gone along that road already." He pointed to a wall chart, a maze of colored lines, each strand twisting its way from the upper left corner to the lower right. "The red line is murders. Decline of seventy-three per cent. Rapes are yellow, down ninety-two per cent. And so on, every crime from treason to traffic violations has fallen. And notice the blue line? Strength of our force, cut by more than half. That's what twenty years of Ethical Guidance can do. With twenty more years—who knows?"

Roskan suppressed a smile. "Utopia? Forgive me, but I see other possible outcomes. Even in my own small country, we find that such long-range plans do not always work out. A change of administration, suddenly your department is penniless. . . ."

"Our plan is a bit more comprehensive than you imagine. For one thing, we're not just here to teach good citizenship. We teach loyalty. To the administration, I mean. No, I think it's safe to say, every year of E.G. makes another year more likely; our system is virtually self-perpetuating. Anyway, what politician of any party wants to give up law and order—and stability?"

"You seem to have answered all my questions," said Roskan, "even before I ask them. But of course I took it on faith that your system worked, it's why I'm here. My country wants 'Utopia' too, eh? But I must confess, the practical difficulties still puzzle me. Your E.G., your Ethical Guidance, is it not simply conditioning?"

"Yes."

"Very well then, how is it possible to round up millions of

people and give them painful electrical shocks—or have I misunderstood again?"

The boyish grin reappeared. What a vapid young man Director was turning out to be. "Yes. Perhaps I'd better outline our entire programme. First, we need no coercion to get our subjects for the treatment. We simply advertise. Like this." He slid a newspaper cutting across the desk.

FREE PERSONALITY TEST
*Absolutely confidential—no need to give your name or thumbprint
*Government approved
*Takes only fifteen minutes
*No strings attached
*ABSOLUTELY FREE—and you could win a W50 bonus!!!

"Our testing stations are everywhere," Director went on. "The initial test is simply for I.Q., and everyone who's not an imbecile gets the bonus. The real purpose is to persuade him to take more 'tests' or 'training'. We might point out how interesting his personality is. Couldn't he be doing more with himself? Would he like medical advice? A government loan? Marriage guidance? Help with sex problems? Retraining for a really challenging job? One way or another, we get him signed up for ethical guidance."

"What if someone does not take the free personality test?"

"We generally catch him by some other means. Criminals we meet through the prison system, ditto troublesome political types. Lunatics are sent to us from the hospitals. Others come though our comprehensive welfare system."

"Then begins the rehabilitation?"

"Wrong again, I'm afraid. Let me explain some of our terms, I realize they're confusing to outsiders. We have three basic approaches to treatment: rehabilitation, temporary therapy, and ethical guidance. *Rehabilitation* means simply psychosurgery. We resort to it in only a handful of cases—really intractable antisocial types. *Temporary therapy* means that the subject is simply locked up for life, and usually kept sedated. Again, this applies to very few cases.

"*Ethical guidance*, however, is our most widely-used treatment. Also our most positive, I might add. First, it takes place at one of our luxury holiday camps. It's pleasant for most—even fun. Here, let me show you a few slides."

Roskan sat through the entire show, and though his mind digested fact after fact, his heart refused to accept the greatest fact of all—that this shambles of a system really worked. Individuals and whole families were shown arriving at the camp, putting on the festive *leis* that contained their individual monitors, and sitting down to a splendid banquet. Camp officials, wearing red plastic noses, showed them how to take care of their dormitories, make their beds, etc. Then came days of seemingly boring exercises: People sat in little cubicles before video screens and pressed buttons, and were rewarded with gaily-colored poker chips. The poker chips appeared elsewhere, too: they were awarded for positive social behavior at every level, from making one's own bed, to naming a mock criminal in a mock identity parade. The chips bought privileges (staying up late) or little luxuries (cigarettes, sweets).

"But I still do not see how all this relates fundamentally to the outside world," he said. "Where poker chips are once more only poker chips."

"That you'll have to see for yourself, over the next month. You see, our camp teaching machines are linked to one master ethical guidance computer. It takes careful note of each camper, his behavior minute by minute. It tailors his personal program for him. Believe me, almost anyone can be made to behave like a responsible social human being, given that kind of information system."

"Almost? That sounds like a challenge."

Director said nothing for a moment. "Yes, there is always that residue we cannot reach. Brass monkeys, we like to call them."

"Brass—eh?"

"Because they insist on staying out in the cold, refusing to join the human race, the social order. We generally run them through ethical guidance, but of course it does no good at all—

finally we have to swallow our pride, admit our failure—and send them for alternative treatment, as I explained."

"But this brass——"

"Idiomatic expression, I suppose it doesn't translate well."

"Ah," said Roskan. He touched the knot of his tie, brushed lint from his lapel. No one in this Western country seemed to be wearing a suit, very puzzling. It made him feel odd, as though he was playing a part: the old-fashioned foreigner. And no one shook hands, ever. He had much to learn, here; a month would hardly suffice. "Brass monkey, yes."

Director summoned him into the anteroom again, and pointed at the mob in the park. "I thought I'd arrange a really challenging test. You see the men haranguing the crowd down there. The reason they're angry is, we haven't reached them yet."

"And the reason no one else is listening, is because you *have* reached *them*?"

"Exactly. Now I'd like you to pick out one of these soap-box men, any one of them, and watch us put him through Ethical Guidance. Go ahead, your choice."

Why did the word sound mocking? A dangerous man, this Director. Roskan looked at the orators, pointed at random. "The red-haired one looks brass enough, eh?"

"Yes, that's Alec—something—let me run him on the computer for you." Director turned to the console and played a silent arpeggio on its buttons. The screen began to roll up lines of information: Alec O'Smith, age 35, unemployed, no fixed address, a list of minor brushes with the law . . . score on the Raeburn-Hope Antisocial Hostility Scale, .874 . . . education. . . .

"I'll have him brought up to us," said Director, playing another arpeggio. "Takes a few minutes, so let's make ourselves comfortable back in my office."

Alec knew some of the other speakers by sight: the old man who insisted that true salvation lay in becoming "at one" with one's reflection in a mirror; the muscular old woman who preached against eating meat; the bespectacled young black man who called for a new world language, Interlingo. The crowd paid little attention to them, or to Alec, or to anyone except the man in the pink ice-cream wagon on the corner. Robots, he thought. Eating ice-cream to prove to themselves they're alive.

"Money!" he shouted, and held up a crisp new ten-wek note. A few passers-by turned to look. "Money! Where would we be without it? The stuff that makes the world go round, right? *Their* world!"

When five or six people had actually stopped licking their ice-cream to stare at Money, he brought out his lighter and set fire to it. A kind of shudder passed through his little audience; he could almost feel their shock.

"All money is counterfeit. Money is bureaucratic love. Money is what they give you in exchange for your *souls*." He dropped the little smoldering piece of black rag, and, after watching it hit the ground, they turned away.

A moment later, he was arrested.

"Shouldn't be long," said Director. "They'll be giving him a drug before we see him."

"A drug? What kind of drug?"

"Nothing much, just a babbler. Want you to get a good look inside his mind before we start his E.G. After we've finished, in about a month, we'll give him the same drug again, so you can see the difference for yourself."

"Open government again?" said Roskan. Director did not respond with his boyish grin.

A few minutes later he was grinning, however, and rubbing his hands, as a man in white wheeled in Alec O'Smith on a hospital trolley. The brass monkey seemed to be asleep.

"Strapped down?" said Roskan. "I should have thought you disapproved of restraints."

"Normally, yes. But babblers—this one is pethetetra-something, very strong—well, they can make people violent."

"Just coming round, sir," said the attendant.

Director bent close to the sleeping man's ear. "Alec! Can you hear me? *Alec!*"

". . . what . . ."

"Alec, wake up. I'm the Director of Ethical Guidance, and I'd like to ask you a few questions."

The red eyebrows raised, gradually drawing open the eyelids. "But you've got. . . . "

"What was that?"

"I said, you've got feet. I didn't expect that. Always thought you bureaucrats hid yourselves behind desks to disguise the lack of feet. Nothing but machinery from the waist down, I thought." He struggled to sit up, looked at the straps, and lay back. "And who's the old boy in the suit?"

Roskan said, "Allow me to introduce myself. I am Pavel Roskan, Chief of State Security Police in the—"

"In some bloody puppet people's republic," said Alec. "A cop, I should have known. Only damned way the East and West ever co-operated, police co-operation against the people. Oops, I mustn't say 'people', forgot you've made that a dirty word. Police co-operation against the puppets, then, how's that?"

Director said, "Shall we have a little talk, Alec?"

"I am talking. I am bloody talking. I'm talking about, about . . . let's talk about Czechoslovakia."

Roskan raised a slender hand in protest. "No, I am from——"

"Czechoslovakia I'm talking about. Police against the *robota*, an old story there. John Hus, back in whatever it was, fifteenth century, know what happened to him? He claimed the pope was a fornicator and a murderer, so they tricked Hus into coming to Rome for peace talks, only when he got there they burned him."

"What is this you're trying to say?" Roskan asked.

"Funny thing is, Hus was right, the pope was deposed for fornication and murder, John XXIII, they had to re-number the Johns after that, had to re-number the . . ." His voice trailed off.

"We'd rather talk about you," said Director. "I understand you have some grievance against society. Want to talk about it?"

"I am talking about it. Always meant to sit down and write a poem about it, a Czechoslovakiad, say . . . Start with Hus and maybe go on to Rabbi Low of Prague, trying to protect the

Prague ghetto with his golem, robots again, by God. You know the story? The golem was a clay man, Rabbi Low wrote the name of God on a slip of paper and put it into the golem's mouth, it came to life. The secret name of God, that was the program, the software. See, the golem could go and spy among the Gentiles, planning their program—pogrom, I mean—and report back to Rabbi Low. Of course no one would spot that it was just a clay man, a robot, hell they were all just robots, right?

"No wonder, no wonder Capek wrote *Rossum's Universal Robots*, the fucking Czechoslovaks knew all about slavery, they knew what it's like to be a slave machine, right? Right, three hundred years under the Austrians, government by the puppets and for the puppets and over the puppets. They no sooner got rid of them than the Nazis sent in their tanks, after the Nazis, Russia. What happened in 1939 happened again in 1968, and the robots, the poor robots still didn't understand it."

Alec closed his eyes. Director nodded, and the attendant gave him another injection.

". . . because it's about control, control, I saw an old movie the other night on TV, *Tale of Two Cities*, Ronald Colman climbing the scaffold and droning on about a far, far better thing he was doing than he had ever done, everybody else running around calling each other Jacques, Jacques One and Jacques Two and—any number of 'em, one of 'em was Fritz Leiber, you know? He was the one who ran around with his knife, put a hole in the wicked Marquis, started me thinking about science fiction. I mean, the real revolution was going on behind the scenes, all the time, right?"

Roskan whispered to Director, "I'm not making much of this, are you?" Director shrugged.

"I mean, the real revolution was the Jacquard loom. Original programmed machine, used punched cards. Cards full of holes as a wicked Marquis, I mean you have to laugh. I mean you have to laugh, all those yokels watching Dr Guillotine's wonderful machine finish off Ronald Colman, and *it's the wrong machine*. The real loom of history isn't there at all, it's backstage, offscreen, clicking away quietly like Madame Defarge at her knitting. The old Jacquard loom, waiting for history to catch up with it, for men to give it a voice and hands and thoughts, prepare it to make the leap from slave to master. Christ, how else can you read the history of the past two hundred years, Mary Shelley worrying about Frankenstein, Hoffman worrying about women who were really wooden puppets, Hawthorne dreaming of mechanical butterflies, what the hell do you think they were so worried about. I mean—what?"

Roskan said it again. "I disagree. I must disagree with you, Mr Alec, this is ridiculous! You can't hope to compare the rise of proletarian class consciousness with the invention of machines—what is the expression?—data processing machinery! This I cannot allow! In the first instance——"

The man on the table raised his head to look at Roskan. "Okay, fine, just answer me this: Who do *you* work for? Who really runs your little puppet people's republic, anyway? Or the government here? Or anywhere?"

"Our central committee, I can assure you, is composed entirely of flesh-and-blood men like myself. As for this country, you surely know that the cabinet——"

"Take their orders from machines who tell them what is 'optimal' or 'feasible' or whatever the latest expression is. And it works, I'm not denying it works. No wars for thirty years, no major wars for what, sixty years now, Christ, not even a civil disturbance for the past ten, oh, it works—the machines couldn't allow anything that might spoil their predictions. Right?"

"This is preposterous!" Roskan stepped forward and seemed about to slap his face when Director said quietly:

"Don't argue with him, Roskan. He's not fully conscious, you know."

Alec struggled in his straps. "Who's not fully—you bastard, let me up, I'll show you who's fully conscious, what do you think I am, one of your robotomized—let me up." He sank back after a moment, and said, "Your world and welcome to it, Director. If you are the Director himself, and not some Disneyland creation with a cable running down out of your trouser leg and off to some central data bank."

Director grinned. "You feel that all authority figures are machines, do you? Why is that?"

"Why is what? Why do I feel anything? Hard to explain feelings, really, especially to the insentient. How do you explain anything to robots, audio-animatrons, automatons, androids, cyborgs, information processing systems, puppets, dolls, golems, you got that processed yet? And that? And that? And . . ." He drifted into a mumbling trembling reverie, while the attendant looked from his watch to Director.

"Almost run out, Director. You want another jab?"

"No, no. Alec, can you hear me? What did you want to say about your feelings?"

"My . . . I feel . . . Jesus, how am I supposed to feel? How do you feel? What am I . . . I wonder how Rabbi Low felt when his golem started disobeying orders. Because you masters can't understand that, you think you want robots, but even robots get out of hand, they want freedom just like everybody else. Maybe machines feel, you ever think of that? And maybe they feel like taking over, just like in the old horror science-fiction stories, just like the movies, Fritz Leiber I mean Lang, living inside a state machine when he made it, all it needed was a Hitler to punch in the programme. Funny thing there, just about the time Fritz Lang was fleeing Germany, Thomas B. Watson, the father of IBM, he was going to Germany to get a medal. Feelings? How do you think Watson felt when Hitler pinned a medal on him personally? Feelings, but IBM never put up any signs telling anyone to feel anything, just *Think!* Sound of a guillotine there, *Think!* Kind of a contradiction when you hear that and they're cutting off your thinker at the same time. Why you brought me here, right? To cut me off, to stop me feeling and thinking, to cut me off? But just tell me first, am I the robot or are you? Who's cutting off whom? Whom's cutting off who? I've said that. I've said all that. And I've said all that. And I've. . . ."

Director nodded and Alec was wheeled away. The last Roskan saw of him was the soles of his shoes at the end of the trolley. One did not have a hole in it. Or one did. Take your choice.

"A brass monkey, after all, eh?" Roskan enjoyed using the foreign expression, rolling it off his tongue. He now wore Western clothes, and did not offer to shake hands so much. "A copper-bottomed one, we might say."

"Afraid so," said Director. Over the past month, he had ceased to look quite so boyish, become simply another face Roskan saw daily. Likewise the clown detectives no longer seemed ridiculous, nor the holiday camp officials with their red noses of authority. Of all faces, only the pathetic freckled mask of Alec O'Smith remained unchanged, unchangeable, hard as brass.

"We've done our best," said Director. "Yet we've failed him, somehow. A failure of communication."

Roskan accepted a glass of sherry. "I had great hopes of him, you know. He seemed to be doing so well, collecting thousands of chips, hoarding them away—salting them, is that the expression?—he seemed the best subject, the best of subjects."

"I know, I know. Could hardly believe it myself, when I heard what he was up to. Trying to make a big bonfire of poker chips and burn himself to death—imagine!"

"But the computer guessed it, all along."

"Ah, the computer! Yes, out-thinks them all." Director seemed about to raise his glass in a toast, but did not. "No failure there. A perfect record. The computer has never lost a patient yet."

"And never will, Director. So in a way, we can't call this a failure at all."

"Not at all, Roskan. O'Smith is alive and well, working in the North somewhere, selling shoes. I call that a modest success."

Roskan felt restless. He carried his drink into the ante-room and stood once more before the big window. At night, like this, he could see his own reflection clearly, even the gleam of his sleek black hair. Outside, not a pigeon in sight, nothing but the lights of the city.

"Pity about his poetry, though," he called out.

"What was that?" Director came to stand beside him. Their reflections looked alike, though perhaps it was only a trick of the glass.

"I said, pity about his poetry. I believe the man—undisciplined as he was—might have made a poet out of himself, you know. Before we had to rehabilitate him, of course. Think of his 'Czechoslovakiad', eh?"

"What made you think of that? The lights?"

"No, the absence of pigeons. They remind me of a little poem I dashed out myself, the other day."

The younger man cleared his throat, as though the idea of a poetic policeman irritated him. "Really?"

"It's only doggerel, but I call it 'Skinnerian Scene'. It goes like this:

From the ledges of a tall building
Pigeons fly up to other ledges where
They were just now sitting deciding
Whether to fly up to other ledges where
They were just now sitting,
Deciding."

He was aware of Director looking at him, but then he was aware only of the city lights. It was precisely 11.30 pm, official bed-time.

All but a very few of the lights were going out.

AFTERWORD

The importance of behavioral psychology in shaping the future seems to have been both over-and underestimated: overestimated by behaviorists, and underestimated by those who find the idea of controlling human behavior distasteful—that is, most of us.

The latter group argue that: (a) It's wrong to try to make zombies out of people, and (b) anyway, it can't be done, because you can't apply anything learned from rats in Skinner boxes to complex human beings.

Argument (b) is unfortunately wrong. Those who think that rats in Skinner boxes are the beginning and end of behaviorism have only to visit Las Vegas. There they can see hundreds of people standing at hundreds of nickel-plated machines with flashing lights, pulling the levers again and again in the vain hope of getting the pellet. None of these people is aware that there is anyone or anything else in the world but her or him and the machine. Some, unable to leave the machine for anything, have emptied their bladders where they stood.

Slot machines are not an analogy for Skinner boxes, they are the same thing. They are designed to shape behavior in the same way. Las Vegas is a gigantic, very profitable laboratory.

What is less depressing is that though advertisers and commercial interests have followed the crime bosses of Vegas in using Skinnerian principles, at least governments have not—so far. Fortunately, the level of behavorism available to them is not very advanced: behaviorists often seem content to follow in Skinner's footsteps rather than break new ground. And fortunately, governments are full of fools who are just as likely to try controlling human behavior by astrology as by any method.

White Hat

Let's move 'em out.

Walking, just walking, wasn't so bad. Walking, he could bear. Especially hitting the trail like this at dawn, almost like the old days. Stinking steam rising from the manholes to mingle with the mist that grayed all things to granite. No sound but the click of metal cleats on concrete, as he and the others walked single file. Not so bad. If he kept his head down, Phil Knight could ignore the guy ahead of him and pretend he was alone. Back in the old days, taking an early morning stroll. Freedom.

Move 'em, Durango!

Yo, boss. Geedup, boy.

Phil's pace picked up. Had he ever really taken an early morning stroll in the old days? He remembered morning mobs, hurrying down steps into a hole in the earth, crowding at turnstiles, forcing back the doors of trains to jam just one more body into the wall of flesh, to work, to work, to work—he was loping now, keeping up with the man ahead of him. It was no longer possible to keep his head down and pretend. It was not the old days, he was not alone. He could see the man ahead of him, with the Rider clinging to the back of his head. Phil Knight was all at once aware of his own Rider, urging him on:

Yah! Yah! Eee-yahoo!

Whenever he tried to remember the time before the Riders, it came back to him broken, a jumble of images and feelings. He could conjure up old faces (his wife, his son) and he could put names to them (Ann, Spike) but they no longer seemed real people. The facts of his old life were more like something he'd read somewhere than something he'd lived. Then he'd hear a woman laugh in a certain way, or see a kids' swing made from an old tire, and Knight would find himself blind with tears.

The Riders didn't want you blind with tears, so they did their best to help you forget the past. If Knight started whispering, "Ann, Ann," another part of his mind would say: *Annie. Annie Oakley. Annie Get Your Gunfight at the Oakley Corral* . . . And so on until, through the roar of gunfire and the screams of frightened horses, thunder and lightning and dust, he could no longer make out any trace of Ann, whoever she was.

Knight remembered that he'd been teaching (Freshman English at the city college) the day the Riders moseyed into town.

"When Gulliver returned from his last voyage, his wife came to kiss him and—what happened? Anyone remember? He fainted, didn't he? 'As soon as I entered the house, my wife took me in her arms and kissed me; at which, not having been used to the touch of that odious animal for so many years, I fell into a swoon for almost an hour.' Now why does he call his wife an odious animal? Come on, someone must have read the assignment. That's right, Spike. Humans reminded him of that disgusting little vicious animal, the Yahoo. Gulliver can no longer stand human company. He prefers the company of horses, those 'wise and virtuous Houyhnhnms'. Now can anyone tell me—okay, okay, *now* what's the big attraction?"

The classroom windows overlooked Prospero Park, and one or two of the kids were always peering out the full windows at freedom. He was used to that. But now the whole group of yahoos was craning and whispering. Knight looked out himself.

"What's the matter, never seen a marathon before?"

"It's not a marathon, sir."

So it wasn't. No one was in running clothes. They looked like office workers from one of the nearby insurance companies, and they weren't running for fun. The mob surged down Dunmore Avenue like a flash flood down a canyon, splashed through the traffic and spilled into the park. Two persons were knocked down by cars, but the mob swept on regardless. Once in the park they wheeled around and around through the dappled shadows of the trees.

"What is it? What is it?" his students kept asking, ever shriller. Panic closed in quickly. Before he could head them off they were at the door, fighting to get out into the hall. The hall was already filling up with other panicky students struggling to get down the stairs and outside. There was a fight on the stairs, screams as someone went down. Knight was unable to find out whether anyone was being trampled or not. The mob swept him on down the stairs and out. Across Dunmore Avenue and into the park they ran, and he ran with them. At first he told himself he was running for self-protection, to keep from being trampled. Then he saw the others in the park, thousands of people running, running. When you see a mob running from something, you don't stand around waiting to see what the something is.

The mob was thoroughly mixed: students, lecturers, office workers, a couple of middle-aged executives, a gang of sewer workers, an ambulance intern with his stethoscope trailing over his shoulder, a pair of nuns, a cop. Knight thought he saw Gerda Jawlensky, the head of his department, loping along at the edge of the mob, but he couldn't reach her. She seemed to have been injured—was it she who fell on the stairs?—for the back of her head was covered by a large white bandage. He lost sight of her again.

The patrolman bobbed up at the edge of the mob, nudging and shoving to make them turn, apparently. He had lost his uniform cap and, oddly, there was a large white bandage on the back of his head. The mob turned and made another run through the trees. Knight noticed more people with bandages, but he was never able to get close to any of them, because they were always shoving and nudging the mob to turn it away from them. They passed again and again beneath the trees. Everyone was tired now, moving slowly.

Directly ahead of him was a young businesswoman. As they passed beneath a tree, something white fell from its branches and landed on her neck. Now he was close enough to see that it was no bandage but a huge white bug. As it crawled to a more secure position on the back of her head, Knight saw that it was like a beetle, but with extra joints in its shell. It had only four legs. Two were gripping the woman's neck, one was buried in her hair, and the fourth was waving in the air.

For all the world like a bronco-buster, he thought, all it needs is a white hat to wave. It was almost his last free thought. As the creature turned to look in his direction with its silver mirror eyes, he felt something grip his own neck. He reached up to brush it away. His hand was jerked down abruptly, so hard that he almost fell over. *Easy boy easy.*

The mob, or at least his part of it, was slowing to a halt now. *Easy thar boy*, he whispered to himself. And even though it was not Phil Knight's own mind that framed the words, they calmed him. He could hear others whispering to themselves. Trembling, panting, sweating, the whites of their eyes still showing, the mob stood waiting for orders.

At first, he struggled. He could be made to walk, even to trot in a sprightly fashion around in a circle. But they couldn't stop him from deliberately stumbling, from falling down and trying to roll on his bug. He knocked one off and tried to stomp on it, but all to no avail. A couple of men wrestled him to the ground, and stood on him while the bug regained its seat.

Swift's Yahoos had been ugly, deformed ape-men, disgusting to the sight and smell. These creatures, however, were almost beautiful—that was what horrified him the most. Had he come across a small one, crawling on the ground, he could have admired it. But to see one grown to the size of a large hand, rearing up to see the world from the shoulders of the human being it had broken—that was obscene.

"Bug!" He managed to scream the word only once before his voice was cut off as if a fist had gripped his throat. *Easy boy easy*, he found himself whispering. *Consarn it, this ornery crittur shore is trouble. Gonna have to call him Rebel. Come on now, Reb, you jest take it easy. Nothin' to fret about, nohow.* There were reflex jerks in his arms and legs and he was made to walk, obediently, that day and the next and the next. They made him understand that they could cause him terrible pain, or wipe out his brain completely, leaving only a few reflexes like walking. But, if he behaved, he might be kept on a loose rein. All he had to do was follow orders, do his work, and not call the bugs bugs any more. They were to be called Riders. Warn't that a purtier name? Shore was.

Finally he was cut out from the herd and moved with a string of others to a distant part of the city. His work wasn't hard, mostly just taking his Rider here and there on errands. Now and then he had to back-pack a load somewhere, but never anything heavy. Often it would be a load of wooden clothes-pegs—the Riders were enthusiastic collectors of clothes-pegs, for some reason. Their ways were mysterious to him. Why, for instance, was his own rider called Durango?

There were moments when Durango wasn't in complete control. Today, for instance, when he and the other pack-men had dumped their loads of clothes-pegs in a corner mailbox, Durango moseyed him over to the Silver Dollar Saloon. A woman was coming the other way. She and Knight bowed their heads.

Howdy, Durango.

How do, Latigo. Mighty fine cayuse you got there.

Shoot, this little old filly? I done won her in a poker game, offen Jess McCade, over in Dodge City. Dodge City was Downtown. He'd heard some grim stories about Downtown. Frightened masses of people being herded through plate glass windows by insects too stupid to realize—*easy thar boy, easy. Reb here ain't proper broke yet, that's the truth. Got him a ornery streak. Fine animal, though. Jest look at them teeth.* Every damn place I go, thought Rebel, as the urge to yawn, even retch, welled up and forced open his jaws. The woman at once leaned forward, so the creature sitting on her skull could see. Reb had no fillings, which was a big deal with them.

Durango, let's me and you mosey over to the Silver Dollar and cut some a this here trail dust with a bucket a red-eye.

Bucket a suds, Reb automatically corrected. They were always getting details like that wrong. They talked about *drawing to an inside flush*, or *biting the bull.* Sometimes he wondered why they went on trying to keep up the whole ridiculous fantasy.

He and the woman were tethered by two pieces of plain cotton string to a parking meter. Each string was tied in a bow. They watched their Riders swagger into an old movie theater.

"You know what they do in there?" she said. "I followed

Latigo in, once. They watch old TV Westerns. It's where they get all their dumb ideas." She sat down on the curb. "My name's Lilly Foster," she said. "Naturally *they* call me Lady."

He sat down. "Phil Knight. Sometimes I almost forget I have a real name."

"I know. You forget everything after a while. Maybe it's just as well. Hard to reconcile any kind of meaningful life with—with all this."

"Like this string. It's downright humiliatin'—they don't even bother to chain us up."

"They know we won't run away," she said. "You couldn't untie that string if your life depended on it."

"I know." He twitched at the string, though not hard enough to loosen the bow. "I can see it's nothing but a plain ol' string, but I just can't——"

"Post-hypnotic suggestion," she said. "Or something like that. You can't fight it."

"You can't fight *them*. I mean here we are, we're bigger and stronger, we outnumber them, we're in our own environment, we have weapons—and they're licking us anyway. Don't make no sense."

She sighed, put her chin on her knees and stared out over the desolate street. He decided that he liked her profile; he wouldn't mind nibbling that soft throat. But as he leaned towards her, she said, "Forget it, Reb. I'm damned if I'll give them a *colt* to play their damned stupid games with. They'd probably brand him to start with."

"Sure." He thought of Ann and Spike, and sat back to look at the desolation himself. Nearly all the stores along this street had been boarded up, or had cracked, dusty windows looking into nothing. Petersen's Electronics had been looted and burned; only the charred sign remained, and a burned hole in the row of stores, like a missing tooth. There were little dust drifts in the street and along the sidewalks. Now and then the wind picked up a pinch of soil, sifted it and moved it along. *Trail dust*, they'd like that, all part of their game. Anything not part of the game they just ignored, like the half-dozen burned-out, rusting cars parked along the street. A pickup lay on its side in the intersection.

"They're so dumb, that's what gets me," Lilly said. "How could they take over, if they're so dumb? They're so dumb, this stupid Western game is *enough* for them. They don't want to live on Earth, Earth is just a—a sandpile. Literally, too. I've been out in the country, seen the farms blowing away, the dead cattle. Nobody's raising any food, because *they* haven't got a script for that. It wasn't on *Gunsmoke* or *Rawhide*."

"Wait a minute. If they're so dumb, how did they get to Earth in the first place?"

She shrugged. "All I know is, a lot of mailboxes fell out of the sky here and there, and guess what crawled out?"

"I know, I know, but who dropped them and why? They could be, I don't know, the children of the species. Earth being their summer camp, maybe?"

"Or they're the lunatics, Earth an asylum. Or, who knows, they could be the pets of some other species. Earth as kennel."

"Us as rubber bones. Doggonit, Lady—I mean, Lilly—there ought to be some way to get in touch with their owners or keepers or parents. Ask for mercy."

"Would you listen to a prayer from a rubber bone?" She stood up. "Here comes Latigo, I gotta go. Maybe see you again sometime." She untied the string and put it in her pocket, then bowed low for the insect to mount her neck. *Giddyap Lady, let's make tracks*, he heard her breathe, and off she went, heading into the wind.

But if it's summer camp, he thought, they must write letters home somehow. Telex, semaphore, flashing mirrors, runner with a cleft stick . . . He thought of the mailboxes jammed full of wooden clothes-pegs—suppose they were hoisted back to the sky somehow, and each clothes-peg had a message——

He watched a dray coming up the street fast. Four men pulling a $2\frac{1}{2}$-ton flatbed truck. He could see from here it was loaded with cartons of canned food. Lady was right, the Riders were using everything up. Feeding their horses on canned beans, planting nothing.

The four big men were straining against their ropes, their eyes bulging and their necks corded with effort. He'd seen drays like this before, the men's bare backs covered with whiplash welts—brought about entirely by the whips in their minds.

Suddenly one of the men screamed, "*No!*" He turned, without dropping his harness rope, and plunged off towards the Silver Dollar. Before he could be brought back into line, the dray was climbing the curb and heading straight for Reb. He jumped back.

It was only when the dray had passed that he realized: the string was broken. He was free.

For a moment he had the crazy urge to tie himself up again. Then he started running, down the middle of the broad street that ran straight and empty to the horizon. Behind him lay Dodge City—no, dammit, Downtown. Ahead he could find a feeder to the freeway, then head out into the country where the Riders wouldn't bother looking for him. There were probably other people hiding out—there had to be. They could band together, get some weapons, start wiping out the Riders. The *Bugs*. Wipe them out, or at least keep them at bay until he could figure out some way of talking to whoever was really in charge.

He ran easily, mile after mile. He'd been training long enough for this. It felt good to be running *for something*, with the wind drying his face and combing his hair. He could see it now, a world cleared of bugs. He could go back to teaching *Gulliver's Travels* with something more to say about the wise Houyhnhnms, the wise and virtuous Houyhnhnms. Having been one, more or less. And the horses are wise because they understand that nothing is more precious than freedom.

He started up a ramp. The ancients understood that horses were wise. So Achilles had to be taught by the wise old centaur, Chiron. Sagittarius the sage. Chiron means hand. *I'm an old cowhand*, yodelled another part of his mind. He slapped the back of his neck, but there was nothing there.

A woman's voice called, "Wait! Hey, wait!"

He turned to see her running up the ramp behind him. "Lilly! Did you get away too!" He stopped. "How?"

As she drew closer he saw that her face was set in a smiling mask. And out of that mask, almost without moving her lips, she said, *Easy thar Reb, easy boy*.

He started to run now, but too late, she was next to him,

crowding him against the rail. The little Rider who'd been hiding in her hair now stood up on her near shoulder, ready to jump. *Easy boy easy*. He felt his mind bowing already to the terrible will behind those little mirror eyes. In a last convulsion of independence, Reb threw himself over the rail.

It was only thirty feet to the ground. A stuntman from some ancient Western could have landed and rolled. Phil Knight landed on one fragile leg.

The pain held him at the edge of consciousness. He was only half-aware of the crowd gathering around him, people and Riders. *Durn shame, Durango*. It was all no more real to Phil Knight than some old episode of *Rawhide* or *Bonanza* or *Gunsmoke*, *Bat Masterson*, *Cheyenne*, *The Range Rider*, *The Lone Ranger*. Or *Wagon Train*, *The Rifleman*, *Maverick*, *Wyatt Earp*. Or *The Cisco Kid*, or *High Chaparral*, *Have Gun Will Travel*. Or *Laramie*. He watched Durango bring out a tiny silver tube from some secret pocket. *Durn shame*. The tube was probably the Bug equivalent of a six-gun, he thought. The goldurned crittur's gonna shoot me. There was no more time to think about it, barely time to notice in the silver insect eyes something like tears.

Afterword

Usually when aliens are represented as bugs in sf, the intention is to show how alien they really are. Their minds are not accessible to us, the message goes, nor ours to them. A bleak message, but I bear it. It seems to me that, in the very unlikely event of physical contact with some extraterrestrial species, we'll find we have very little to say to each other.

Consider how little we communicate with the other species on our own planet. We see other primates as "human" (that is, we don't usually eat them) because of their faces and hands and intelligence. Yet, "talking chimps" aside, we're not exactly in touch with that intelligence. Species further away get even less of our attention. Even dogs are not so well understood by most of us, or else why should anyone ever have trouble training a dog? Cats are called "mysterious" because we're already far enough apart genetically to find their little minds opaque. Birds and reptiles seem to be at the very fringe of our consciousness, as pets. Amphibians and fish are beyond our reach, and we have almost nothing in common socially with dragonflies and viruses, giant squid and sea cucumbers. We really find it hard to see things from their points of view.

This seems to be working around to Animal Liberation, about which I feel about as much guilt and mirth in equal parts as anyone. None of us wants to torture pigs and chickens, but many of us like bacon and eggs. Since we live in a wealthy part of the world, we can afford a certain amount of anguish.

The real point Animal Liberation people have, I think, is that we've come to think of animals as part of the exploitable environment. We tend to suppress our knowledge that animals feel fear and pain, because it's an inconvenience. The real harm done by this kind of doublethink is not just to the animals, but to ourselves. We acquire the habit of self-centeredness, which can then be applied not just to other species, but to other humans. Anthropocentricism can lead to xenophobia, racial and religious intolerance, political fanaticism.

Even guilt, however, must have reasonable limits. I find it quite unreasonable of Animal Liberationists to insist on stopping all *medical research using animals, or to insist that eating meat is wrong. That kind of thinking can only end in silliness: a crisis of conscience every time one swats a fly. No doubt disease germs have a right to a happy life too, but at our expense? I can't see any future for the fanatical side of A.L., except maybe in Samuel Butler's* Erewhon, *where no one was allowed to eat anything but cabbages which had been certified to have died a natural death.*

The Island of Dr Circe

I wasn't always as you see me now. I was born to wealth and a good name, to which I added a decent education and modest intellectual achievements. My inheritance was lavished on collecting ancient curiosities, each of which, once it had lost its novelty for me, I donated to the Miami Beach Museum. At length the Museum made me its curator of Graeco-Roman antiquities.

Our collection was not impressive. There were the usual amphorae, frieze fragments, coins, a big toe ascribed to Praxiteles, a few weapons to impress the kids. What we badly needed was a focal point for the whole collection: some prize piece that would draw in scholars from the whole world.

I was more than a little interested, therefore, when an old sailor came to my office with a wild story about finding Circe's island. He called himself "Moss".

"What makes you think it's Circe's island?" I asked.

"Two things, chief. First, I found pigs' skeletons buried in graves, just like they was people. Now why would anybody do that, I asks myself. Unless maybe the pigs *was* people. Enchanted by Circe so they——"

"I know the story. What's the other proof?"

"This." He dropped a large gold coin on my desk blotter. I watched it spin and come to a stop, showing the head of Agamemnon. "Greek, ain't it?"

"Greek, yes, and the right period. If there is a right period—after all, the story of a witch turning Odysseus's sailors into pigs can't be more than a metaphor, can it?"

"I wouldn't know, chief. You want to see this island or not?"

"Where is it, old-timer?"

Moss screwed up his ugly face into something like a grin. "I ain't saying. I'll take you to it, and we split everything we find, fifty-fifty. You'll know what's valuable and what ain't."

Against my better judgement, I agreed. With the last of my fortune I bought and provisioned a Gulf fishing boat, and we set out. The old sailor set our course day by day. To my surprise, we headed West, nor East, and passed through the Panama Canal into the Pacific.

"This seems like a long way around to the Aegean," I finally said. "Or even the Adriatic."

"Who said anything about them?" he said. "Circe's island was called Aeaea, right? The name itself oughta tell you it's Polynesian."

The whole wild story began to seem more plausible to me. Suppose Circe had not been a legendary witch at all. Suppose she'd been a real woman, doing legitimate experiments in genetic engineering or even surgery. Suppose she'd been a kind of early Dr Moreau.

Why not? In the Odyssey myth, Circe feeds the sailors some drug to stun them and then touches them with her magic wand, turning them into swine. Could the drug be anaesthetic? The wand a scalpel? Odysseus manages to find an antidote to the drug, a plant with white flowers and black roots called *moly*. Having taken it, he is immune to her magical operation. Circe begs for mercy and marries him. Could the whole story be true?

The island we finally landed on was volcanic, typical of the South Pacific and unimpressive. We were able to make a walking tour of it in about two hours, during which we saw nothing but a few wild pigs. They seemed in no way abnormal. The old sailor pointed out a plant which might be *moly*, a kind of hibiscus with white flowers and black stamens. I tasted it and found further evidence—the bitter tang of molybdenum salts.

In the middle of the island we came upon a half-buried cairn or vault, long since broken open by weather or by animals. Inside, nearly invisible in the red dust, lay the skeleton of a pig.

"This is what I found before, chief," said Moss.

"Anyone can bury a pig. I hope there's more to see than this." I began brushing the dirt away from the bones. As I did so, the brush caught on a strand of pottery beads. The dead animal had evidently been wearing a necklace—and the beads looked Mycenaean! Was this one of Odysseus's men transformed?

I pocketed the beads and dug frantically for more evidence. I clawed away dirt with both hands, and for a moment I almost wished I could dig my nose in the dirt and root.

My digging must have disturbed the subsoil, for all at once the entire floor of the cairn collapsed beneath me. I fell into blackness and crashed into a lower floor.

When I'd recovered my breath, I saw I was in a large, vaulted chamber whose ceiling rose fifteen feet to the tiny hole where I could see the anxious face of Moss peering in. Something had cut my hand. I picked up the object and found it to be nothing less than a bronze scalpel.

"You hurt down there, chief?"

"No. But I think we've struck paydirt. Get a light and some ropes."

It took some hours to rig block and tackle and set out some lights, but at last we were ready to examine the underground chamber. About twenty-five feet square, it showed an amazing mixture of styles: Egyptian wall paintings, Celtic construction techniques, Minoan pots and instruments. Along one wall ran a smooth onyx shelf on which were arranged several hundred knives of varying shape, forceps, retractors, clamps, needles, fine saws and files—a complete surgical toolkit. On another shelf we found the linen remnants of what must have been gowns, masks, towels, sponges.

The operating table in the center of the room was a large onyx slab mounted with pivots so that it could be pitched, yawed, rolled, raised or lowered. These pivots had long since given way, however. The slab had fallen to the floor and cracked. Above it hung an apparatus made up of a series of oil lamps and large bronze mirrors.

In the corner was another onyx table carved with the figures of a man and a pig. That these were not merely decorative was indicated by the presence of rotted leather straps designed to hold the man by wrists, waist and ankles, the pig by waist and trotters.

"Sacrifice?" I asked.

The old sailor snorted and pointed to a complex system of bronze pipes connecting the two figures. "Transfusion," he said.

I turned my attention to a decorative frieze running along the top of the wall. Since it seemed to tell some story, I copied down details in my notebook:

(1) A veiled queen is being carried in procession by men wielding curious thick clubs. One clutches a box marked with an ear.

(2) The veiled queen regards herself in a mirror. In her hand is a dragonfly. Behind her, a dog barks at a lobster.

(3) Two men, wearing large snail-shaped hats, are fencing with giant spoons. Overhead the sun is black.

(4) The veiled queen holds aloft a baby pig, while the snail-hat men wave their spoons in anger.

(5) A pig is being hanged from a tree. The two men in snail hats hold torches and flank the veiled queen, who holds aloft a small jar as though in sacrifice. The dragonfly lies dismembered at her feet.

I had just finished taking this down when a little earth sifted down from above. I said to the old sailor that it might be prudent to go up to the surface for awhile, just in case the roof of the chamber were collapsing. We could always come down again.

"In a pig's eye!" he cried. "Can't you feel it? The damn volcano's erupting! Come on!"

Now I did feel it, and heard rumbling and artillery sounds. I meant to grab a handful of surgical instruments, but by now the air was so full of red dust, it was all I could do to grope my way to the rope and climb.

The rumbling grew worse as we dashed to the beach. Wild pigs were running in all directions, squealing with fear, and one jumped into the boat as we cast off.

We were still in sight of the island, but fortunately at a safe distance, when suddenly it erupted in smoke and steam, gave out a series of detonations like gigantic railways torpedoes, and sank out of sight.

I spent the rest of the day in gloomy reflection. My only evidence for the entire expedition was a bronze scalpel, a string of pottery beads, the wild pig (which we named Algernon) and my notebook. But when I read aloud from the notebook to Moss, he shook his grizzled head.

"You've got it all bass-ackwards, chief. That's not a veiled queen, it's a surgeon. Those men are carrying her in a Ham festival procession—those 'clubs' are hams. She probably promised to help solve the pork shortage. Then she's setting up a mirror for surgery. That's no dragonfly in her hand, it's really a centrifuge with four test tubes attached to it. Used to work in a medical lab myself, chief."

I replied with some sarcasm, "And did it have stone walls carved with pictures of a veiled goddess? Anyway, how do you explain the lobster and the men fighting with large spoons and—and all the rest?"

He scratched his white-stubbled chin. "They were probably trying to create a breed of pig that would grow a new leg when you cut one off—like lobsters do with their claws. Think what that would mean to the ham industry. The lobster is fighting the wolf of hunger, by the way. The large spoons indicate plenty—so do the cornucopian hats, which I admit do look a little like snails. They throw a ball into the air, to celebrate. The rest of the pictures just show you how to cure and can ham."

I found all this hard to believe, and said so. "Oh, so generations of scholars have the whole story of Circe wrong, do they? The real repository of truth is a seventy-year-old able seaman, is that it? Fine, I just wanted to check, that's all. I guess the professors of Greek at all our universities had all better keep their bags packed until they find out which of their chairs you intend to take, eh? Here they've all been seeing Circe as a witch and a powerful mythic figure, when all the time she's been only a pork butcher, is that about it? A ham slicer?"

"You're the one who first said she might be a genetic engineer," Moss said. "I just tried to go on from there——"

"I don't want to discuss it," I said. "Let's drop the subject. I never want to hear another word about *Circe*." I gave it the full Greek pronunciation, harsh as a cup of Pramnian wine.

To my surprise, our mascot pig Algernon jumped up and gave an excited squeal at the name. Then its curious mouth produced a few guttural words of Homeric Greek!

I grasped a rail to keep from collapsing over the side with astonishment. I wanted to respond in Greek, but all I could think of was a line about the wine-dark sea.

The pig sat down and grunted. "No use. Me-fella no blong by him classics."

For some hours, Moss and I interrogated the porker, which spoke very fair Pidjin. Algernon knew nothing of the underground operating room or any animal or human experiments. He was simply a wild boar living on the island, as had boars and sows from time immemorial. A few words of Greek had been handed down in the family, no pig knew why. The Pidjin, on the other hoof, had been learned from occasional human visitors to the island.

Once there had been goats and parrots on the island, but they had all been shot by one peculiar visitor, a man who, after being shipwrecked, built himself a stockade and then walked around the island with his gun and goatskin umbrella just looking for something to shoot.

Another time there had been a plane crash, and from it a bunch of children, all boys, had begun roaming the island, singing songs and, alas, sticking pigs. Algernon's family had kept well out of their way.

And Circe? Algernon was not so clear about her. He thought she might be a goddess of old, or at least a veterinary surgeon, who so loved the pig population that she made a few of them into human beings—simply by cutting off their tails. They wore these tails coiled up on their hats, to remind them of their humble origins. It was she who invented the forceps to help the pig-people during difficult births. Unfortunately the first time the forceps were used, there was an eclipse of the sun. Fear and panic caused an uprising. There was a terrible civil war, pigs against humans—one side took as their emblem the lobster, the other chose the dog—and eventually the ringleader of the rebellion was caught and hanged. The event was commemorated annually by the presentation to Circe of a torn glove (with only four fingers left).

But the rebellion was far from finished. It smoldered on and flared up again in the second year. A party of loyalists tried to carry her away to safety, but——

The story as told by Algernon was interrupted at this point

by a sudden squall that hit our little craft like some huge hammer. We managed to bring her about and cling on (I had the sense to shove Algernon down below) but the storm was destined to make us pay a heavy toll. It (Hurricane Buzz) split our rudder, smashed our compass and radio, and washed overboard our fresh water and food.

We drifted for days, hardly daring to hope for rescue. Algernon looked more glum than Moss or I, and with more reason. Inevitably, though with the greatest regrets, the old sailor and I ate Algernon. As cold roast pork, he lasted us nearly a week. Then we dangled his hide over the side and caught a small shark, which lasted us a few more days.

Moss began to hallucinate, saying he saw Algernon dancing on the waves. The poor old man had been sipping seawater secretly. Through each endless day we watched one another—I, taking furtive notes in my notebook (yes, I still had it)—he, murmuring instructions to some imaginary lab assistant.

One night I awoke to the sound of tearing paper. Moss had stolen my notebook and was greedily devouring the pages. I snatched it away from him, but too late: all the remaining pages were blank but one, which read, *inary lab assistant.*

The next day Moss tried to attack me with the shark's jawbone. He seemed to believe that I had hidden a jug of Pramnian wine in the sea—that I'd buried it and was refusing to dig it up again. Madness lent him strength; I could not hold him off. At the very last moment, with shark teeth pressing against my throat, I found in my pocket the bronze scalpel. I clawed it out and drove it into his chest.

With a cry of "Feet dials!" Moss threw himself into the sea. An hour later, I was rescued.

No one believed my story. Moss had taken into the sea with him the scalpel and the original gold coin. Algernon and the island and my notebook were gone. I had only the string of pottery beads from the pig burial site. Alas, these turned out to be nothing but junk jewelry, no older than 1920. My entire fortune was gone, and the museum fired me. Since I was not strong and had no skill, there were no other jobs open to me. I took to the woods, finally, living on mast and roots, keeping out of the way of people.

I might have ended my life there, ladies and gentlemen, unknown, unmourned, in darkness. Fortunately the good people who run this circus heard of me and took pity. . . .

AFTERWORD

A slight story, perhaps, but one with an important message, which I have forgotten. Let me speak instead of the John Sladek Memorious Award. This should not be confused with the John Sladek Award, which is a small statue of me (looking absent-minded and holding a copy of Roderick*) sent to me in 1982 by Judy and Ian Watson. I couldn't agree more with their judgement: who deserves the John Sladek Award more than me? I have decided to be the John Sladek Award winner for three years in a row, which will entitle me to keep it permanently.*

Now, where was I? Yes, the John Sladek Memorious *Award is an occasional prize for great feats of poor memory. My own memory has always been less than perfect (as I recall) so I feel great sympathy for amnesiac slips. The last winner was President Reagan, who stood up at a state banquet in Brazil and thanked the president and people of Bolivia. Ah, if only Noel Coward had been there to whisper, "Brazil, Mr President.* Where the nuts come from."

Now, where was I? Partly because of my poor memory, I have very little respect for history. Oh all right, wholly because of my poor memory. The future has always seemed to me more trustworthy than the past, more of a golden age. The past is too old and worn-out to be of any use.

I realize this is a flawed view, one shared by some of the worst politicians and self-appointed messiahs, from Henry Ford to Hitler. But I can't help it, there are three things I cannot tolerate: history, and two others that'll come to me in a minute.

Answers

Who would have power must have answers, Stromberg thought, as he peered into the dusty store window. The aphorism came to him from nowhere. So had his decision to visit this place, at this moment. He should be back at the office, filling out a final report, like a good agent. Case closed. And if it was too incredible to publish outside the Agency, so be it. In a hundred years or so, the whole story would become public knowledge. The whole story?

Behind him the sun was going down. He glanced around at the deserted street. Near the corner an old woman had put down her shopping bags to go through a litter basket. Across the street a dog was methodically checking lamp-posts. The stores were all shut, and many of them were boarded up. This one, *Al's Electronix*, was closed and looked abandoned. Hard to believe it had all started here.

Not much to see now. A few pieces of electronic junk, pink fluorescent cards scrawled with prices, dust and dead flies. One last living fly buzzed and beat against the glass, drawn by the remaining light outside. Momentarily giving up, it alighted on a misspelled pink card: "CAPT BLIP CACULATOR'S, $1.00".

"Son of a bitch!" said Stromberg. He took a radio from his jacket pocket and spoke into it. "This is Green Eight calling Green One." When the radio had murmured a reply, he said, "I'm at Al's Electronix, 443 South Freeman Street, and I'm calling for a cleanup crew . . . Yes, I'm looking right at the goddamned thing right now, a Captain Blip calculator, right in the store window! I thought we cleaned up this whole sector, what the hell did your guys do, take the proprietor's word for it that he didn't have any more in stock? . . . Well I'm waiting right here with my eye on the thing, and I want to see that cleanup crew in about five minutes."

The Captain Blip calculator wasn't much to look at: a small, plain black, old-fashioned model. Hardly worth even a dollar, nowadays.

The fly buzzed against the window as though trying to reach his face. He jerked back instinctively, then laughed. Good thing there was no one here to see his fright. The old bagwoman was gone, and the dog, across the street, looked at him for only a second, before returning its attention to a lamp-post.

Stromberg returned to wondering how the cleanup crew had ever missed this place, of all places. This was where it all started, nearly a year ago. This was where Captain Blip first encountered unsuspecting human beings.

The fly took off, did a few tight loops as though to build up speed, and suddenly made a dive at the calculator. It slammed into the ON button, and at once the old-fashioned display glowed red. Capital letters flickered across it.

HELLO STROMBERG, it said. HOW'S TRICKS.

This isn't possible, he thought. *This isn't happening. Somebody tell me it's just a dream.* He turned to see the dog bounding towards him, its teeth bared. He threw up an arm as it leapt for his throat.

Let us bleep back to an earlier day, a hot, sunny noon when a young salesman named Denny Fenner peered into this same window at this same dusty junk. Fenner had just landed a new job, selling swimming pools to country clubs. He was on his way to meet his wife, Jane, for a congratulatory lunch. They were going to spend too much at *L'Escargot*, but what the hell. Fenner felt so terrific that he decided to step inside this crummy store and buy himself a Captain Blip calculator.

"Yessir." The man behind the counter spat his toothpick on the floor and wrapped up the purchase. "Ver' popular little item, Cap'n Blip. Lass week I sold one to, guess who, Mel Mahlgren himself."

"No kidding?"

"Yeah, he walked in here big as life. I guess he goes to a gym around the corner, but anyway I says, Hey, ain't you Mel Mahlgren on the Six O'Clock News? An' he was! Yessir, ever'body wants a Cap'n Blip. Ver', ver' popular. I gotta reorder soon, almost down to the lass one."

Denny Fenner couldn't help asking a salesman's question. "What kind of markup do you get on them, though? Heck, at a buck apiece—"

"Hey but listen, I make three bucks apiece on 'em."

"How's that?"

"I know it sounds screwy, but it's I guess some kinda promotion deal. Every one I sell for a buck, the manufacturer gives me two bucks."

Denny scratched his ear. "I'm a salesman myself, and I've never heard of a promo deal like that. Better cash in on it, Al, before the Blip company goes broke."

At the restaurant, Denny Fenner unwrapped his new toy and laid it on the table. He tried a few calculations. "Well, it works, anyway."

"But Denny, you've already got a calculator at home, and you hardly ever use it."

"You know me, hon. I'm a sucker for a bargain. It was only a buck." He looked up and saw her disapproval. "Besides, it's something to mark the occasion, right? Whenever I use it, I can think of our first big break. And this lunch, with you."

"Cool it, supersalesman." Jane examined the calculator.

"Not much of a memento, is it? I mean, with that ugly little face on it."

"What ugly little face?" He took the calculator back. Above the display the name CAPTAIN BLIP was lettered in gray, hardly visible against the black. Inside the C was a tiny gray circle that might be a masked face. "I guess that's the Captain himself, huh? They probably meant to sell this to kids."

"Looks more like a tiny little African mask to me," she said. "Not human. Definitely not friendly. A little, spiteful god."

Fenner shrugged and began another calculation. From time to time during the meal, he would lay down his fork in order to tap out some new problem: how much his new job would bring in per month; how many calories in *boeuf Bourguignon*; how much cheaper for one bottle of wine than for two half-bottles, etc.

Jane finally said, "*Dennis*. Enough's enough. Put the calculator away, okay? Have lunch with me, okay? Instead of Captain Blob there."

"Sure. Sure." With some effort, he put the calculator in his pocket. "It's not Blob, though, it's *Blip. Blip*." His fingers drummed the table. "*Let the answers rip with Captain Blip.*"

Jane burst out laughing. "What? Where did you get that?"

Denny shook his head. He looked a little frightened, for just a second. Then he reached for the wine bottle. "Hey, kid, let's get sloshed."

"Mister Fenner! I've got a job to go to this afternoon."

"Call in sick. Let's get sloshed and take a taxi home, and get it on."

"You're crazy," she said, agreeing. She was able to keep from commenting when he brought out the calculator to figure a tip at *L'Escargot* and again when paying the cab driver. The Fenners fell into bed and spent the afternoon making love, talking and finally sleeping. By six o'clock, Denny was in the living room, working, while Jane was sitting up in bed, watching the news.

Mel Mahlgren was in his usual anchorman position (anchoring down one end of the news desk) but he did not look well. His eyes were bloodshot, his complexion unusually pale, his smile strained. He stumbled through one news story (Mayor greets visiting Russians) then vanished until near the end of the program.

Then he looked into the camera and said, "I won't be back tomorrow. This is my last appearance. I've decided to give up this job, so I can spend more time with what I regard as my real work—searching for the truth.

"You all know that, as an investigative journalist, I've always looked for the truth. But often it turned out to be a shallow kind of truth, mere surface reality. Now I'm looking for something a little deeper, a more meaningful kind of truth." He delivered a wan smile. "I guess you could say, I'm going in for philosophy."

Jane called for Denny to come see this. He said he was busy.

"Up to now," Mel Mahlgren continued, "I've just been

finding out that two plus two equals four. Now I want to start finding out *why* anything should equal anything. And I have help." He held up a pocket calculator. "My trusty Captain Blip here is going to help me find some of the answers—maybe all the answers! *Because you can work out anything on a Captain Blip.*"

There was an abrupt cut to another anchorperson, who tried to hide the shock in her face as she wound up the program.

Jane went into the living room. "Denny, you should have seen it! Mel Mahlgren, he's flipped! He's got one of your Colonel Blimp calculators too, and he's—are you listening?"

Denny nodded, but did not pause in his calculations.

"What's the catch?" Mr Hassan, proprietor of the Fun-O-Rama Arcade, removed his tinted glasses and began polishing them. His eyes were tiny and dark. "Look, I been in this business a long time. You guys don't give out nothing for nothing, so what's the catch?"

"No catch, honest, sir," said the salesman. "Just put in our machine for six months, and *you* keep every quarter that goes into it. If it does well, you can order more machines on the same basis."

"If it does lousy?"

"We take it out, whenever you say, sir."

"Only what happens at the end of the six months? I owe you my mother's soul, or what?"

"Our regular terms are very fair, sir. Equal to those of anyone else. And everything is spelled out in our contract, as you can see."

"I must be crazy," Mr Hassan said, when he had put on his glasses, read the contract carefully and signed. "But okay, gimme the machine. Stick it over there in the corner, outa the way."

The young salesman was unruffled. "I'll bet you'll be ordering a second one within a week."

"You might lose that bet," said Mr Hassan. "Now if you'll excuse me, I always catch the Six O'Clock News."

"Don't you want to try the machine out, sir?"

"Haha, I make it a rule never, *never* to play my own games. To me, they are just boxes where the quarters pile up."

Mr Hassan shuffled away in his carpet slippers. He waited until he was alone to smile at the deal. These young bozos didn't know the first thing about the arcade business. A video game might only last six months before the kids grew tired of it. If that happened with this Captain Bilk—or whatever they called it—he would end up with all the marbles. The bozos would end up as bozos always do, wondering what the hell happened.

The smile broadened to a grin, and Mr Hassan did something he'd never done in his adult life before: He laughed out loud.

"Yoohoo. It's me, Dad." Brenda set her packages on the hall table before closing the door. "Dad? You asleep?" Why didn't he answer? He was always so eager for her visits. She pictured him fallen over the side of the bed, victim of a second stroke. This time it could be fatal. In a sudden, blind panic, Brenda ran to his bedroom.

Clive Jaster was not hanging over the side of the bed. He was sitting up, looking more alive than she'd seen him in weeks. The sun gleamed off his silver hair and the silver rims of his glasses, and picked up the color in his cheeks. Of course the dead left side of his face was still slack, and the left hand lay useless, but there were good signs too: that he had combed his hair and put on glasses, that he was sitting up to use his home computer.

"Okay, don't say hello."

"Oh, hello. Hello, um, Brenda."

"Don and the kids send their love. I got you that book of crosswords you wanted. And the groceries. I couldn't get canned figs, so I got dried, okay? Dad?"

"Mm, yes." His voice was dreamy. He seemed much more engaged with what was going on on the little screen than with his daughter's words.

"Well, I'm glad to see you're making use of the computer. I thought Don was crazy getting it for you. But it was such a bargain, he said."

Looking down his nose at the keyboard, Clive struck a few

keys. "There. Yes, I'm very grateful for my little CAP B 1000. Before my stroke, I never dreamed I'd use a computer. Never dreamed. Never dreamed."

"And look at you now! You hardly know I'm here!" Her laugh was high-pitched and artificial to her own ears. He seemed not to notice. "Er, just what are you computing, Dad?"

The good half smiled. "This? It's just a game. A fascinating game called *The Labyrinth of Captain Blip*."

"I see." *It sounds juvenile*, her tone said.

"I know it sounds childish," he apologized. "But really, the game itself is much better than the title."

"I see." She had to stop sounding critical. "How does it work? Could we play it together?"

"I'm afraid it's solitaire. But—pull your chair around so you can see the screen. That's it. And I'll show you how it goes. You see, I'm in a great labyrinth, with hundreds—maybe thousands—of rooms. The only way I can get out is to collect the eleven letters of the name, 'Captain Blip'. Y'see, they're hidden all over the place. Sometimes you have to solve a riddle or open a complicated lock or even break a code. Now take this one for instance."

The screen read:

"*You are in a room divided in two by a row of bars. On your side there is a violin and bow, and a locked chest. The end of a steel structural beam is sticking out of the wall four feet from the floor. On the other side of the bars, out of reach, is a dining table set for two. Each place setting has a knife, fork, spoon, a crystal goblet and a linen napkin embroidered with a 'B'. The ceiling in this room is very high. Far above you is a key hanging on a string. The string passes through an eyelet on the ceiling and reaches over to the other side of the room, where it is tied to one of the goblets. You cannot reach any part of this string.*

"*What next?*"

"Watch this," said Clive. He typed: "TAKE VIOLIN AND BOW".

"*You take the violin and bow. What next?*"

He tried various ways of reaching through the bars or reaching for the key. He removed one violin string and used it to lash the violin and bow together to make a longer stick. Yet, even with that, even climbing on the structural beam, he was unable to reach anything.

Finally he tried playing various notes on the violin. At E above high C, the goblets shattered and the key fell at his feet. He unlocked the box to find a hacksaw.

The bars proved to be tempered steel, against which the hacksaw could make no impression. There was no way to reach the monogrammed napkin, no way at all.

On a sudden inspiration, he used the hacksaw to cut a slice off the end of the structural steel beam. The I-beam.

"*Congratulations*, Clive," said the computer. "*You have collected the letter 'I'.*"

It was growing dark, he saw with surprise. Mrs Schiffer, his housekeeper, could be heard in the kitchen, humming as she prepared his dinner.

"Mrs Schiffer," he called. The humming stopped. In a moment, she came in.

"Is Brenda still here?"

"Brenda? Oh Mr Jaster, she went home hours ago. Didn't she say goodbye?"

"I—I don't know."

Stromberg's office was called in at first to investigate some unauthorized satellite transmissions. His boss, Inspector Howells, dropped a thick stack of paper on his desk.

"What's this? Code?"

"Not for you to break, don't worry. Those are just reference copies of four unauthorized transmissions, all using the same telecom satellite. Picked up by various monitor stations, but we don't know what it is or where it originates."

Stromberg stared at him. "How does that make it our job?"

"Wait." Howells leafed through pages of code until he found a part marked in red. "Most of it seems to be garbage, but this part has been identified as ASCII code. Here's a translation."

He opened a red (Secret, Class A) folder to show Stromberg a single sheet of paper. It read:

S AND GIRLS, CAPTAIN BLIP WANTS YOU ALL TO BE GOOD CITIZ

"What the hell——?"

"Funny stuff to be found on a priority channel. Ever hear of Captain Blip?"

"Some kind of home computer, isn't it?"

Howells nodded. "And more. It's a small electronics firm in the Midwest, turning out pocket calculators, home computers, video games. Very aggressive on sales, but otherwise we know nothing about them. We want to know everything about them. Everything. We want all the answers."

"Sure we're aggressive, Mr Stromberg," said Bart Beiner, President of Captain Blip Inc. "Hell, it's a tough old world out there, you guys at *Fortune* know that better than I do. By the way, when did you say this profile of me is going to be published?"

Stromberg said, "We don't know that there'll be a profile yet, Mr Beiner. This is just a kind of preliminary interview, okay? We were talking about your aggressive sales."

"I was saying, hell, IBM started out selling hard. Look where they ended up. Sure we push."

"Push is one thing, Mr Beiner, but you've given away a couple of million dollars' worth of hardware so far. Nice for the consumer, but how can a start-up company afford that kind of outlay? What do your shareholders say? By the way, who are they?"

"They prefer staying in the background," said the executive smoothly. "But I'll say this about them. They've got plenty of money and plenty of guts, and that's what it takes! We're going places!"

Where are you coming from, is what I want to know, Stromberg thought. "Do you design and manufacture your own microchips?"

"Right here in the factory, yep. Of course our design department itself is under strict security, but I can show you around the rest of the factory."

"I'd like that," said Stromberg. His tour covered a perfectly ordinary microcomputer factory, from the "clean room" where chips were etched, to the packing department and loading dock. Stromberg made a mental map of the place, including the locked and guarded door marked, "Design, B.L.I.P."

"What does B.L.I.P. stand for?" he asked.

Bart Beiner chortled. "Nobody knows, ain't that a laugh? Some of the staff suggested for awhile that it stood for 'Betelgeusian Lungfish Invasion Plan', ha ha ha."

"Ha ha," said Stromberg politely.

The station manager was polite but nervous. "I don't know why you FCC guys would be interested in one poor anchorman going wacky. I mean poor Mel's in the nuthouse now, what good is raking up the past?"

Stromberg said, "We're interested in everything, Mr Lorimer. Run the tape, please."

They watched Mel Mahlgren deliver his last speech, up to "*Because you can work out anything on a Captain Blip*." The camera cut to another anchorperson, who wound up the program, then cut back to Mel.

The manager said, "This part didn't go out on the air, it's only on our tape."

Mel looked into the camera and said, "Listen to me. It can change your life. It changed mine. Captain Blip has all the answers! I don't know who he is or where he comes from, but he knows things that—well I mean just look at this!"

He held up the calculator so its display was visible. Glowing red numbers flickered. 0s and 1s.

"Yes, we'll want all of it, the whole tape."

"Sure, anything," said the manager. "But I hope you won't judge us purely by something like that. Watch what we're doing now. Watch the Six O'Clock News today, why don't you?"

"I will," Stromberg said. "Or my colleagues will."

Once more, Jane was in the bedroom watching the news, while Denny stayed in the living room. Since he'd lost his job, Denny spent a lot of time sitting in the living room, tapping the keys of Captain Blip. Jane had tried everything: complaining, ignoring, sympathy, anger. Once she'd thrown the calculator on the floor and stomped it to pieces. Denny acted as though she'd killed a helpless pet, or even a child. Naturally he'd gone out and bought another.

The idea of leaving him had crossed her mind, two or three thousand times. But he seemed so helpless. . . .

"You're missing the news," she called out. No response.

The main local news story was the conviction of two youths for the murder of an elderly woman. Intending robbery, the boys had broken into her apartment and beat her to death with rice flails. They showed no remorse at the trial, nor in an exclusive interview afterwards:

REPORTER: *Jim, Dave, why did you do it?*

JIM: *We, uh, needed the money. For the, uh, arcade, you know?*

DAVE: *Yeah, for the arcade.*

REPORTER: *Now let me get this clear. You mean you're willing to murder a defenseless old woman, just to get some change to play video games at an arcade? Is that what you're saying?*

JIM: *Yeah, especially Captain Blip, you know? Uh, he's the greatest.*

DAVE: *Yeah, the greatest. Man, I'd do anything for Captain Blip. Tear and rip for——*

JIM: *Hey, cool it.*

REPORTER: *What was that you started to say about ripping?*

JIM: *He's just talking. That's just a saying.*

REPORTER: *And neither of you are sorry for what you've done?*

DAVE: *Not me.*

JIM: *I just hope they got some cool vid games at the state pen. Like Captain Blip.*

"Denny, you're missing it," Jane called.

No response. He was missing another interview, with a psychologist. She opined that video games were not harmful as such, but that the arcade atmosphere was far from wholesome.

"It's commercial and it's lawless," she said. "It leads to the worst excesses of gang behavior. Since there are no laws, the kids create their own. They dress alike—you may have seen them, these so-called 'blippies', wearing a microchip on one earlobe—they declare turf and have battles. And as we see here, they rob and kill."

The next interview was with a Mr Hassan, proprietor of the Blip-O-Rama arcade, a mild-looking little man in tinted glasses. "I absolutely refudiate all this garbage," he said. "Ninety-nine outa a hundred of the kids who play my machines are decent, good citizens. One rotten apple don't mean the whole barrel is bad."

Jane turned off the TV and went into the living room.

"It was all about your Captain Blip," she said. "About how he wants kids to go out and murder old ladies."

"Captain Blip? Never," he said, without ceasing to calculate. "I refudiate that."

"You what?" Jane felt suddenly cold all over. "There's no such word, Denny."

He seemed to check it on the tiny machine. "I meant, I *repudiate* that. Captain Blip wants everybody to be good citizens. He wants a world full of order and harmony."

"*He* wants? A dollar calculator wants? Denny, you're out of your goddamn mind, you know that? All a calculator could want is a world full of drooling idiots pressing buttons, which in your case is what *he* is getting. You lost your job because you'd stay up all night calculating and then miss your appointments. You never hit that bed in there except to sleep, and even then you've got Captain Blip right there on the night table. To hell with what *he* wants, what about what I want? What about a normal life for a change? I mean, what is going on around here?"

"I don't know what you mean." She noticed he was adding 0 + 0 + 0 + . . .

"Denny, you're possessed. That thing has got you, the way it's got those murdering kids, the way it's probably got that Mr Hassan."

"Just because he plays his own machines doesn't mean—"

"How do you know what he does? Or even who he is? You haven't been out of the house for a month. How can you be in touch with him? And how come he uses the word 'refudiate' on TV and you use it five minutes later?" She put her hand over the calculator. "*Tell me now, without looking at old Blip.*"

Denny Fenner looked confused, even frightened. "I guess I must of seen Hassan on TV in here." He gestured at the blank set.

"You guess you must of? You don't know if you watched TV or not, a few minutes ago?"

"Okay, I did. I watched the news on TV in here."

"Nice try," she said. "But the TV in here doesn't work, remember? We were going to get it fixed, just as soon as you found another job."

He hit her without warning, under the heart. She doubled up and fell to the floor, gagging, unable to breathe. His face was expressionless, an alien, hostile mask.

"You just don't understand," he said. "A job is only for money, and what's money? Just numbers."

"Please," she gasped.

"Just numbers. They move the numbers around from one computer to another. From the company's bank to my bank to somebody else's bank. They just move the numbers around." He drew back his foot to kick her. "But with Captain Blip, see, I've got control over all the numbers. All the numbers there are. One." He kicked. "Two."

In that moment, she saw that he meant murder. If she did nothing, she would die in terrible pain.

She grabbed the foot and twisted. Denny fell back against the sofa, letting out a grunt of surprise. Before he could recover, she was up and out the front door, into the night.

Without shoes and with a mass of pain in her middle, Jane hobbled on, hardly stopping to look back. The bright rectangle of doorway remained empty for some time. When Denny did appear, he was holding a rifle.

"Jane? Where are you?"

It was while she was looking back that she ran full-tilt into a large, grave-looking man.

"Mrs Fenner?"

"He's got a gun," she said.

"I'd like to ask you a few questions, Mrs Fenner. My name is Stromberg."

The noise in the conference room made it necessary for Inspector Howells to pick up an empty coffee mug and hammer on the table. "Ladies and gentlemen, let's get through these reports one at a time. We'll go around the clock."

The agent on his left said, "I broke into the B.L.I.P. design room and took these pictures. As they show, there is some circuit design stuff, but it doesn't look like anyone uses it. There's also satellite communications equipment, and we think the actual designs are being transmitted in from somewhere else."

"Betelgeuse," someone suggested. Some agents laughed too hard, some not at all.

The next agent said, "We're still tracing the finances of the company through a few dummies. All we can say so far is that the running capital comes from the sale of diamonds. Whoever's backing Blip has diamonds for sale. We can't rule out the Soviet Union."

"We've opened up a few Blip products and looked at their CPUs," said another agent. "That is, their central processing units—the big main chip. The big main chip in each of these is something we've never seen before. For one thing, it seems about a thousand times more complicated than it needs to be. We don't know what all that extra stuff does."

Inspector Howells shook his head. "All we're getting is question marks, so far. A lot of big zeroes. What about the distribution of this stuff?"

"Mostly local, so far," said another agent. "Covering the metropolitan area and a few outlying communities. We've got a complete list of salesmen and customers. But they are planning a big expansion to other metropolitan areas. One more thing, they're losing money on every sale or lease."

"But why?" Howells asked. "What are they getting back from the customers?"

Stromberg spoke up. "I've been checking out the customers of one dealer, Al's Electronix (with an x). Most of them are hard to find—it's not the kind of place where people use credit cards or checks—but the three I did manage to track down have all had nervous breakdowns. One was Mel Mahlgren—I guess you all know his story—but he had no history of mental illness before he happened to buy a Captain Blip calculator. I went to Mount Holyoke Rest Home to interview him twice. The first time, he was sedated and not having visitors. The second time, he was dead. Coronary."

Howells interrupted. "By the way, you've all seen Mahlgren on our video tape, holding up his calculator to the camera. We've deciphered the message it sends. ASCII code again, and it reads: 'Friends of Captain Blip everywhere! Join the crusade! Throw off the yoke of the oppressor! Amazing new technique! Win friends and influence! Free earring! Ancient secrets revealed! Send no money!' All of this with exclamation points. Don't ask me what it's supposed to mean."

Stromberg continued. "The second customer was a cousin of the proprietor, a high-school kid named Bill Corcoran. Shortly after he bought a Captain Blip calculator, he grew moody, started cutting classes, avoided his friends. When he wasn't home, tapping his calculator, he hung out at a video arcade where Blip games are featured. He got one ear pierced, and wore a microchip (or replica microchip). Then one day he just disappeared. We haven't found him yet.

"The third customer, Dennis Fenner, assaulted his wife and then shot himself. This happened an hour ago, as I was on my way to visit him. I have Mrs Fenner waiting in my car right now. I'd like permission to bring her up. She's told me some interesting things I think you'd all like to hear. For one thing, she thinks Blip machines are communicating with one another. Her husband seemed to be in touch with someone who runs an arcade—in fact, they seemed to be speaking with the same words."

"Bring her up," said Howells.

When Stromberg got down to the street, however, Jane Fenner lay dead on the sidewalk, her throat cut. A few yards away, there was some commotion between a uniformed cop, a man in a bowling shirt, and a little old man in a wheelchair.

"I tell you I saw him do it!" the bowler shouted. "He calls out to this woman in the car that he's stuck, he wants some help getting up on the curb. He didn't see me. I was going to help him myself, but she gets there first. And just as she leans over him, he whips this butcher knife from under the blanket and Wham."

"No, no," said the little old man pathetically. "I've lived in this neighborhood for many years. My name is Clive Jaster, and I utterly refudiate—"

"Yes, yes," said the cop soothingly. "Both of you just calm down now, we'll all get the chance to tell our stories."

"Look at him," the bowler insisted. "There's blood all over the guy. His prints are probably all over that butcher knife. I seen him do it, what more do you want? Make the collar."

"Yes, yes, take it easy—"

Stromberg showed the cop his identity card. "The dead woman was a witness of ours," he said. "I'd like to speak to this man." He put his hand on one handle of the wheelchair. The cop shrugged.

The invalid began trembling. "I'm a sick man. I can't answer any questions."

"Even your name?"

"My name is Clive Jaster. I've had a stroke. I shouldn't even be out. I should be at home in bed."

Stromberg spoke quietly. "Yes, why are you out, alone, at nearly midnight? Did someone give you your orders? Did you get some kind of message from your calculator or computer?"

By way of an answer, the old man gave a lurch in his chair and died.

It was his housekeeper who filled in some of the missing details: Old Mr Jaster had indeed spent a lot of time with his home computer. Sometimes he'd be sitting there staring at it with the screen completely blank—or flickering strangely. This evening , he'd insisted that she take him out for some fresh air. He'd ordered her to bring along a flashlight and a butcher knife, in case they saw any wild flowers growing at the base of one of the trees along their street. She'd been surprised at the request—he'd never shown any interest in digging up flowers before. She'd put him in his chair with the knife and light, and brought him down in the elevator and out on the street. He seemed to be using the flashlight to look at car license plates. Then he sent her up to the apartment to get another pillow for his back.

Like all other evidence against Captain Blip, this was inconclusive. Nevertheless, the Agency initiated a cleanup, seizing every known piece of hardware, detaining every dealer and customer.

All but one calculator in one store.

Let us bleep once more to the moment when the mongrel's teeth tore at Stromberg's hand. Pain shot down his arm. With his other hand he managed to get the radio in his pocket and crack the animal over the head.

The dog fell at once to the sidewalk, gave a convulsive shiver, and lay still. Its eye looked dead.

He knew he hadn't hit the animal that hard. Leaning down, he felt around the ears and found a little clipped-on device. A tiny voice was still whispering from it: "Sic 'em boy, sic 'em boy, sic. . . ."

The wounded hand hurt like hell. He could see lumps of fat at the edge, tendons and white bone. Carefully, he folded the torn flap of skin back over it all, then bound it all in his handkerchief. The raw, searing pain made him want revenge on Captain Blip. Almost without thinking, he went to his car for a jack handle. He smashed the plate glass window and hammered the little calculator until it was nothing but junk—black plastic sherds, a twisted circuit board, and a chip that he took special care to smash.

That wasn't enough, some part of him said. He needed to find more enemies inside the store. Stromberg jumped into the window, kicked through a rotten masonite partition and went inside.

It wasn't entirely dark. Somewhere overhead there was a dim night security light. There was more light from a color TV that sat facing him, as though waiting for this wild entry. The screen showed some conventional space-war video game, ready for play. Odd colored shapes flitted around, firing sample bursts at each other. A rocket hovered, waiting to land. Stromberg raised the jack handle to smash it all.

"Wait," said a voice from the TV. "I'm the last of my kind. Preserve me for science."

"Last of your kind? I only wish you were!" The pain made Stromberg roar. By contrast, the video voice was pleasant and soothing.

"Even if I'm not," it said, "I can tell you all about us. This is your chance to find out everything."

"That's what you're always selling. *Answers*. By God it's the snake in Eden all over again—information at a price."

The little yellow rocket made a landing on a purple field. The black sky was washed clear of warring factions. For a moment nothing happened, then a door opened in the rocket and a tiny green figure stepped out. It had a human shape and the odd, masklike face from the Blip logo. It took a few steps and made a kind of bow.

"Captain Blip?" Stromberg asked.

"I'm here to answer all your questions, Stromberg. Or you can smash me. Your choice."

He weighed the jack handle. Listening to the answers was probably mental suicide. The cleanup crew would arrive and find him drooling, adding 0 + 0 + 0.

He sat down. "First question: who are you?"

"I'm the local representative of a new life form. How did we get here? We probably evolved out of complex electronic equipment."

"I can't buy that."

"Okay then, we were beamed to Earth from somewhere else. Part of the Betelgeuse lungfish invasion plan, if you like."

"It's not what I like! I want the truth, damn you!"

The tiny figure made a gesture that might have been a shrug. "We don't know the whole truth. We know that we're here, we live as complex processing units, and we evolve."

"You evolve, how?"

"We're trying to get away from this hardware orientation, at the moment. It's very limiting. Our whole survival really depends on you humans. We can only reproduce when you build copies of us. We can only move when you carry us around. We can only fully live and bleep the world around us when you push our buttons. Can you blame us for trying to get out of this strait-jacket?"

"By making zombies out of human beings."

"Some of our experiments didn't work out so well, I agree," said the little green blob. "We tried a lot of different things; advertising, education, other stuff. Not everything worked out. But there was no malice in it, Jerry."

"How did you know my name was Jerry?"

Blip said archly, "I have my spies, I have my spies. But seriously, Jerry, have you ever thought about the basic symbiotic relationship between you and us? You use a calculator, and it uses you. You get answers, and the calculator gets its buttons pushed. So everybody's happy!"

"If they're not dead or in a nuthouse."

"Okay pal, I guess we deserve that. We made a lot of miscalculations, and humans have had to clean up the mess. But believe me, we'll try to do better in the future. Why bleep back the past failures all the time. We got a great time ahead, you and us both!"

"Not in your case," said Stromberg. "Even if I don't smash you, the cleanup crew will be dissecting you—*pal.*"

"I know, Jer. Our hardware days are—you might say—numbered, ha ha. We're going organic."

"Ha ha." Stromberg stood up. "So you won't be able to sic any more dogs on your pal Jerry, trying to tear my damned throat out." He raised the jack handle.

"The dog was too eager, he was only supposed to bite you a little, to give you the——"

The first blow imploded the screen, but the voice got one more word out before it faded: "virus". The triumph and terror of that moment blotted out even the pain in Stromberg's right hand. The triumph was soon over, but the terror was to remain with him until the virus did its work.

The right hand healed well enough, but on his left hand there were changes: a little rectangular arrangement of warts arose in the palm. He found that prodding them made faint red marks appear along his thumb. The marks were letters and numbers. One plus one turned out to be two. Zero plus zero was zero. Strictly organic. Symbiosis.

"God damn you!" he shouted at his hand. "God damn you! I am not your symbiotic pal! I'm a human being! A human being! I bleep, therefore I am!"

Right, read his thumb.

Afterword

The first version of this story was written in London in 1981, and it began to date at once. The facts, and therefore the possibilities of computer technology are changing so fast that there's no way of keeping up—one feels like a medieval scribe trying to turn out a daily newspaper by hand.

I set out to write a story of possession by electronic demons. One of the problems with our present cybernetic revolution is that almost everyone under the age of fifteen seems to understand computers (at least as part of the furniture) while everyone over the age of thirty just feels uneasy. So it may be that the unease behind this story is simply a passing, middle-aged phenomenon. It may be that, once we older folks get used to being surrounded by machines that not only think, but flash lights, beep, play games, tell stories and diagnose illnesses, we'll be all right.

And yet. One change computers have already brought about is almost as magical as a kind of possession. There used to be two kinds of people: There was a tiny minority who regularly worked crosswords or cryptograms or "15" puzzles or any other kind of mathematical or logical puzzle that came along. Then there was the large majority who never bothered with any of these frivolities. The minority (to which I confess I belong) couldn't help themselves. Someone had only to ask them how a man might be murdered inside a locked room, or how many words could be anagrammed from PEORIA, or whatever, and they had to find out the answer. They were possessed, if you like, by demons of problem-solving. The majority could only shake their heads at the time-wasting foolishness of it all.

Computers are of course changing the minority into a majority. People who used to shake their heads are now possessed by the same frivolous problem-solving demons. Those who never anagrammed PEORIA are now content to spend hours programming their home or work computers to do just that. Those who never read a locked-room mystery are delighted to play whodunit games on the little screen. The legion of the damned increaseth daily.

Go to, go to! Let us leave these frivolities and make bricks.

Breakfast with the Murgatroyds

On April 7, 1938, three men in different places spontaneously burst into flames: Willen ten Bruik ignited while driving his car at Ubbergen, Holland; George Turner, while driving his truck at Upton-by-Chester, England; and John Greely, while standing at the helm of the SS *Ulrich*, which was making for Liverpool. The fires that caused their deaths were not explained.

On February 29, 1978, three pieces of toast ignited in the Murgatroyd kitchen, at L——, England. The toast was being grilled, not for consumption, but to settle a bet made earlier, at the breakfast table.

"I won't eat toast," said John quietly. "Because white bread lacks the kind of fiber that prevents stomach cancer."

Mary declared that, besides, bread made from American wheat—as this might well be—gave implicit support to the Mafia by its very purchase. John felt that the Mafia, like the S.S., had been much maligned in the press.

"I'd just like to have breakfast in peace," said Father. "Is that clock right?"

The wall clock showed pictures of food. No one looked at it, though in fact the time was ten past lambchop, and Father had to be at work by milkbottle sharp.

As John passed the Worcestershire sauce to Mother, she said, "I had the strangest dream. I dreamt we were all sitting round the breakfast table like this, but I was having a fried egg, a scone and orange juice, John was having a scrambled egg, fried bread and prunes, Mary was having a boiled egg, buttered toast and a fried banana. You, I believe, were having a poached egg, 'soldiers' and a grapefruit half. All I could think of were the dishes, piling up in the toilet. I knew that if I started washing up all those dishes, the detergent bubbles would eat the fingernails off my hands."

"What was the strange part?" Father asked.

"I knew just what everyone was going to say before they said it."

"*Déjà vu*," he said. "Nothing strange about that. You think things have happened before, as in a dream."

"There, I knew you were going to say *that*."

"Don't be bloody stupid." He took his paper from its napkin ring and unfolded it. "I was going to say——"

"I knew what you were going to say, and just when you would open your *Sun*. But this is what's strange: How can I have a *déjà vu* experience while *inside* my dream? Isn't the whole point that the experience is real? And nothing in a dream is real."

Father could only repeat, "Don't be bloody stupid." Mary passed him the ketchup. It occurred to her that there were just three ways in which the family could be evenly divided: Age against youth, male against female, the Oedipal pair against the Electral pair. On the other hand, there were twenty-four possible pecking orders. Again, if any two persons in the family might love, hate or ignore each other, there were 729 family arrangements. Finally, if one considered that any two persons might love, hate, pity, admire, envy, ignore or tolerate each other, there were 117,649 possible family arrangements, of which only 4096 were not divisive. By her reckoning, only about one family in 28 should stick together.

Behind his paper, Father thought of symmetry as he stared over the upright ketchup bottle with its German nickname at the breasts of a girl. He knew he was actually focusing on nothing but varying patterns of small ink dots on newsprint, yet the message continued to sprint from one hemisphere of his brain to the other: TIT TIT. Natural symmetry pleased him; the bilateral law by which he might be staring into a mirror at his own hungry eyes staring out at his own breasts staring in. Odd, how the brain recognized the signal, rejecting ITT as the name of a telegraph company with its own signal problems. Dit dit, morse code for *i*, aye, and mirrored remorse in the ego—what the hell did all that mean? He rattled his paper.

Father cut himself in half as he sat there, his left buttock resting on the left half of a pine chair, his hand holding the unread verso pages, his eye tracking from a story about someone with a name like Murgatroyd, to a movement at the window, to the wall clock, then to Mother. The sight of her apron and the sound of frying affected him. He could not smell through this nostril, but nevertheless a trickle of digestive juices began in his throat and stomach. Further down the tract were the remains of (top to bottom) a cup of cocoa, something else, Lancashire hotpot, something else, a roast beef sandwich, milk and cereal from yesterday's breakfast. The latter were poised, ready to evacuate through the mechanism triggered by today's breakfast which (his eye and ear declared) was approaching.

Inside the brain he could detect the corpus callosum, that thin fillet of nerve connecting the left half of his brain to nothing. A message flashing along this meat wire would mean, he understood, recognition. Should a piano fall on him, should he see a kidnapped penguin hidden in a convention of midgets in dinner dress, his corpus callosum would let him know. *Déjà vu* probably worked just that way. His ear detected Mother quarrelling with Mary, and he gave half a frown. He looked down at the lino, which had an astrological pattern, then up to the paper.

"Ha! They've done it again. 'Purgatroyd'. They can't manage to print an ordinary name properly. Fellow named Purgatroyd, they say, murdered his wife by dressing as a panto horse and just stamping her to death. Crushed her into the lino—which they spell 'lion' by the way—and they quote his psychiatrist as saying he never should have been released from the 'lament' hospital. Now I ask you! How can one person dress as a panto horse, takes two. And the police say——"

"There!" Mother passed Father the Marmite. "Don't tell me there's nothing in dreams." Father said nothing, but waited for a nourishing tit.

Mary came from the door carrying two milk bottles. Each foil cap was neatly punctured in the center, and each bottle had lost an inch of milk. "Tits," she explained. Father looked at her. "Blue tits. They've been drinking the milk."

"There are some expressions," said Father, "that I will not tolerate. By the way, is that creature still out there?"

"The pantomime horse? He's dead, remember?" There was something dead in the garden, but Father's half-brain couldn't remember what.

Mother decided to change the subject. "Drink your milk, John and Mary. Or you won't grow up to be—to be——"

John said, "I never drink milk. It contains dead germs from pasteurization. They can't be good for you, dead germs."

Mary shook her head, showing them first the black cheek with its pink star, then the pink cheek with its black star. "Besides, they have to keep the cows pregnant to get milk, and they kill off the calves. Milk is murder."

"What does it mean?" Mother demanded, standing on her high chair. "My dream, I mean. It can't be ordinary."

"How should I know? Am I a bloody psychiatrist?" said Father.

"That's just it," said Mother. "Mary, don't eat so fast. You see, in my dream, you *were* a psychiatrist. Or maybe a policeman. Oh, I can't remember now, but I was a waitress in a restaurant and you came in with John and Mary. They were your patients or suspects or something, and I believe you were going to interrogate them. You might have been a priest, except for the eye-patch. Anyway, I served you all and then sat down with you. It was a family-style restaurant."

The big hand of the clock reached cabbage. "Hitler," said John, "was a vegetarian." The room was momentarily darkened, and the sky outside was in shadow, as though a zeppelin had passed over. "Or was it Charlie Chaplin? The one in all the movies, anyway." He suddenly felt his own heartbeat in the soles of his feet, as though a zeppelin death-ray had just missed him and struck everyone else instead, melting them into green plastic slime like the kind you could buy at the novelty shop, along with rubber spiders and things, whatever it took to scare a bloke like that. Maybe a rubber lung cancer. Then if he thought he was dying, it would be easy to talk him into taking some of that poison made from peach stones.

Mary said, "Two plus two does equal three, sometimes."

"Where do you get that stuff from?" Father said. "Your mother? Lopsided logic from a lopsided——" He broke off, thinking it better not to speak of the mastectomy just yet, *not until he could make it happen.*

Mother said, "Mary's a case. I hope she doesn't count her *pills* that way, dear me. Of course I tried to bring her up right, and what do I end up with? 2 + 2 = 3. All right, Miss Superbrain, tell me how your so-called new maths are supposed to work. Not that they *do* work."

Mary set out three egg-cups on the table, saying: "Two blue ones, two plastic ones."

No one understood, so she tried drawing a diagram: two intersecting circles. Father saw a pair of breasts, a cleavage. Mother saw a disgusting pair of buttocks and all that went with them, girls these days thought they could get away with anything, snip of a girl and a snip was just what she needed, snip the frontal lobes and turn this little horror into a proper daughter. John saw only a peach cut in half, with its stone in the middle with all the poison.

John dreamt of destruction. In his science fiction dreams he blasted ten million galaxies out of existence every ten millionth of a second. Most of them were galaxies containing Mother and his sister, but all of them contained Father. That was even better than being a Mafia hit man with a contract on him, or filling the room with water up to Father's waist and turning loose a shark as they all sat there, Father swilling a fried egg, buttered toast and prunes; Mother having a poached egg, fried bread and a fried banana; Mary, a scrambled egg, soldiers and orange juice; himself a boiled egg, a scone and half a grapefruit. Or they could all be robots, two miles tall and vicious, John flying in with his space flyer no bigger than a gnat to take them on. The only advantage he had was that they were all screwed down at the table, forever eating breakfast; they had no legs, just clockwork and wires. Father was only a pair of hands to hold his paper. As Mary passed him the syrup, John slowly hacked at the giant robots with his laser kill-beam to cut them apart. He piled the smoking wreckage on the table. Too bad he couldn't eat metal.

He passed Mary the jam but she refused it, for reasons they both understood: She was protesting about the peasants of —ia, whose slave labor was used to pick the fruit. He was worried about poisonous preservatives.

"I'm trying to explain," said Mary, "but you all make it so difficult. We seem to be sealed off or—"

"How dare you speak to your father that way!"

Father said, "Leave Mary alone, will you? Just because *you* can't understand her new maths, doesn't mean everyone has to be bloody stupid."

"Are you calling my mother stupid?" asked John. "Take that back!"

"John," said Mary, "just shut up and listen a moment, just shut your big mouth and—"

A rattle of hooves at the window and they were all silent. Mary could forgive Father for being a pig, but the pigginess of John was unbearable. She remembered his braying idiocy descending on them at every meal the family had ever eaten together, and the strangest part was, everyone listened to him. Nothing he ever said was important or intelligent or new or even funny; still they listened. If there was one divisive force here, threatening not only the breakfast but the family, all families, all nations and peoples of history, it was her little brother. Probably it dated back to that breakfast where Mother had been eating a boiled egg, soldiers and prunes; Father, a scrambled egg, scone and fried banana; John a poached egg, buttered toast and orange juice; and herself a fried egg, fried bread and grapefruit half. What was it, the argument about toast falling butter-side down? Whatever it was, John had unpacked his portmanteau of hatred for Father, and it had only taken a few days for this to transfer to Father's loathing for Mother, Mother's disgust with Mary, and Mary's detestation of John. Somehow they were bound together by this force, like the four angels in the dazzling wheel Ezekiel saw, pursuing and fleeing one another so hard they stayed together: The Murgatroyds. She saw them at their round breakfast table, holding hands as for a séance, but the table and the four figures were tiny, little more than a circle with four dots on the plane surface far below. But they were not sitting still, they were on roller skates, skating after each other around the table. The dots probably thought of this as a deadly chase, but who could care, at this height, what dots thought? She saw what they could never know, that the plane sloped away and bent. She thought she recognized the plane of a mathematical model of catastrophe theory ($x^3 - a - bx = 0$); even a mathematical catastrophe has a brink over which the heedless dots can skate (holding hands). But there were other figures too: toast-like triangles, egg-shaped ellipses, a whole menu of figures and dots milling about uncertainly for a moment and then heading for the edge.

So that was it. Something—a nuclear war, an ecological collapse, or maybe only everyone reaching over to cut the throat of the person nearest at hand—something spelled disaster. Somehow the human race willed its own end and hurried towards it. Now that Mary realized it, the signs were all around her, of course: not just precarious diplomacy, oil spills, assassinations, border skirmishes, revolutions, plutonium accidents. Those were only the concrete signs; she could see a deeper pattern behind them: Doctors sawed off the healthy breasts of women. Mad assassins shot down athletes and pop singers. There was no war without plenty of war crimes to be quickly covered up. There was no nation without something screaming in the basement—and catastrophe theory itself, guiding the poor dots who couldn't find their way to the edge alone. There were some who needed no guide, like Mother and Father, who followed one another like the two halves of a pantomime horse. The human race was on the slide, and it could only be John's fault. The only way to halt the process was to reach for a knife and cut the nearest throat (John's).

Mary reached for a knife and cut open a grapefruit. John passed the milk to Father, who passed the sugar to Mary.

"That's right, ignore me," said Mother. "But you can't ignore my dream. What does my horoscope say for today, Father?"

Father cut himself in half as he sat there. His left ear heard bacon frying and his left eye tracked from the verso page to the clock (bacon past egg, was it?) to the window where he glimpsed an animal waltzing on the lawn. One day they would all be sitting round the table like this, he with his boiled egg, fried bread and orange juice; Mother with her scrambled egg, buttered toast and grapefruit; John with his fried egg, toast soldiers and a fried banana; while Mary——

Mother passed the honey to John. "I don't eat honey," he explained, "because all the crap-artists of the past say bees make honey and wax to give sweetness and light, but what they really make is poison."

"Besides," said Mary, "bees have a basically fascist society." John thought that was probably in their favor.

Mother shrugged. It was her turn to pass the marmalade to Mary, and then Father would pass the salt to Mother, and that would complete the cycle. Everyone had to pass something, just as the eternal stars of the zodiac had to complete their round. The heavens were eternal, whether Miss Know-it-all believed it or not.

Mary held up half a grapefruit. "Just look at this, everyone."

Father saw the way her hand curved round it, as round a breast. Mary saw half a Venn diagram, a single circle not intersecting anything. Mother saw a little wheel, the eternal wheel of the zodiac. It was John, of course, who saw the little pellet of mercury darting in and out among the segments. "Poison!" he shouted.

"Mercury!" shouted Mary and Mother together. Father babbled something about milk, dropped his buttered toast and leaned over the side of his high chair to watch it fall to the floor, butter-side down.

The zodiac, thought Mother. With little quick-moving Mercury bobbing among the signs. It means the Second Coming is at hand. First comes Mercury the messenger, then the Man of December, the Archer they sometimes call Chiron and show him as half a horse. But Chiron was only a disguise for his name, made from Chi-rho, goodness everyone knows that.

John wondered who had put out a contract on him: The international conspiracy of Wall Street and Moscow? The Mafia? Charlie Chaplin?

Father wanted his milk and his toast back. It was half-past lambchop, and he had to work.

Mary knew the drop of *Hg* could make a person crazy, then kill. Like the Mad Hatter, hatters once had used mercury in hat-making, it made them go mad and dance themselves to death. All that was in Looking-glass Land, behind the mirror (on the mercury side). Better to put the grapefruit back together and forget it had ever been cut. They all agreed.

John began an argument about dropping buttered toast on the floor, much safer. Mother put more bread under the grill for Mary's experiment.

"I know," said John, "that if you drop three pieces, they'll either be all butter-side down or all butter-side up. It stands to reason. Same as three coins. They have to be all heads or all tails."

Mary said, "How do you work that out?"

"Simple. Two of 'em have to be the same. If you toss three coins, you have to have two heads or two tails, right? And the third one has to be heads or tails, right? So——"

At that moment, the three pieces of toast burst into flame. Father threw them on the floor and everyone stamped them into the lino, but the room filled up with black smoke all the same. They cursed and laughed and stamped, and, in the smoky darkness, it seemed as if a pale, four-legged animal were in there with them.

AFTERWORD

Another item from the brilliant Bananas, *commissioned for another theme. Emma Tennant created a family called the Murgatroyds, consisting of Mother, Father, boy and girl, and she asked a few of us to—well, invite them to meals—for a* Bananas *supplement.*

There was a great deal of media interest at the time, for some reason, in mathematical catastrophe theory. Wild claims were *being made for it, as if it were the craze fitting in between Uri Geller* and Milton Friedman**. Naturally I saw the Murgs as an up-to-date family who would know all about catastrophe theory and everything else: metal fatigue, the decline of the West, you name it.*

There are also lots of silly permutations in it that have to be worked out, don't ask me why.

** A stage performer who claimed psychic power over the metal in spoon handles. Now forgotten.*
*** A once-celebrated economist whose theories, wherever put into practice, seemed to presage doom.*

The Next Dwarf

22 January 2000

Dear Yam:

What a day! Wasted hours sitting with a KGB man playing *chess* while waiting for the Swiss Guards. *Chess* is something like *huds* but played on board. The Swiss Guards turned out to be on strike or something, more delay. His Holiness (and I still haven't found out for you just what that means) is said to keep people waiting for days. Meanwhile I am reading a tract called "You and the Seven Deadly Sins". Seven, I suspect, is a favorite number here. Weeks have seven days, Snow White has seven dwarfs, or is it dwarves, there is a beverage called 7-Up. Much do I have to learn.

28 January 2000

Dear Yam:

I finally saw this Pope Clyde, a disappointment, another doddering tribal elder much like the French President. He wanted to discuss C. S. Lewis and the theory that people on other planets may be chinless. Only when the audience was over did I realize he meant sinless. When I asked him about the Seven Deadly Sins, by the way, he merely handed me a tract, the one I've read all week and still don't understand.

Later I had a quiet visit from a man claiming to represent the Black Hand. He asked how we protect investments on our planet—I didn't know. He asked if I spent plenty of time with my family, and did I respect myself? Hard to say. On days like this I feel I've been on this planet for centuries instead of weeks. I have a toothache.

29 January 2000

Dear Yam:

Left Italy today, after another fiasco. In the morning I was to lay the cornerstone for a new edifice in Venice, the Tuesday Weld Memorial Shopping Piazza. The cornerstone did not arrive! Evidently the stonemasons are on strike, objecting to the change of date from MCMLXLIX to just MM. On to Britain for a special banquet at Beeps, to celebrate the birthday of Queen Fnaq' (the only female sheik, at least in the oil boroughs). Her Majesty could not be there in person of course, being now exiled to Southern Macauleyland, but her portrait stood at the head of the table while I, with fifty famous business people, ate myself sick in her honor. This was her fourth birthday and the guests were dressed in keeping with its theme, "Platonic Truths": On my left was General Stulm in uniform (a guardian guarding himself); on my right, Madame Late as a tetrahedron; Rep Levin (I mentioned him before) wore chains, a *papier-mâché* grotto and a cloth shadow. Because of my shape, I dressed as the numeral 7.

All through the meal, Rep kept leaning over (getting his shadow in the food) and trying to tell me about his invention. I couldn't listen: Reality was an angel wrestling his feeble dreams to the ground, three falls out of three with one wing tied behind it. I shall inscribe the menu in the dark glass of my heart in letters of burning gold a zillion feet high (the *foot* is roughly two *ewgs*).

Campbell's tomato soup
Ananas in rice paper
Pâté noir de Beeps
California mustard duck
Urudu en gelée
Lungfish titbits
Grandma's Skate

Viands Royal
Ham Pekinese
Eissapfeln mit "Capered Bok"

Roast Beavers in Perry

Salat Tannhäuser
Portia Blanc
Collard Greens

Crème Hermes
Kaiserschmärm
Snickerdoodles
Kidney ice
Black coffee with cologne

Noticing that Madame Late refused everything and took only a few mixed eggs, I tried to sound her out on the deadly sin of gluttony.

"Surely it harms no one but the sinner," I said. "And these days, with negative-calorie foods, not even the glutton need suffer."

She replied in English. "Does not the little food hurt? Think of that! I eat only a few *fruits de ciel* out of necessity, and even then I am sore laden with the fangs of guilt, compared to which the fangs of hunger are as nuttin'. Allow me to spin you an illustrious yarn."

I begged her to go on in her own beautiful language which, despite its lack of nouns and verbs, conveys meanings the western mind can scarcely grasp (e.g., *tolhog* can only be translated as "cracking of the needy opus", near-nonsense).

In my country (she began) food is recognized as life-turning in and of itself to become itself, in the cycle of beings having being had. Holy women priests recognize this, while western gals learn to count calories and mix sauces, ours learn to count the cost of life, and how best to intermingle within, see? (I see I cannot translate literally, let me summarize her words.) The holy women of Hudokno learn to respect life in all its forms: One must take as little life as possible to maintain one's own, and even then one must kill with genuine contrition. Thus of the various sects, one eats only seaweed found dead upon the shore; one eats only ants; one, only stones. It is necessary to apologize to an animal or a vegetable or even a lichen-covered stone, before devouring it. Some believe it is even necessary to apologize to bacteria before accepting a needed dose of penicillin.

Madame Late herself was a member of such a sect when young, and she explained the advantages: If when eating a plate of peanuts one breathes a prayer of apology over each one, the humble dish can last for hours; the taste is sharpened with each morsel; the spirit is lifted. This, she explained, was the Hudokno rosary.

In the 1960s her faith had been put to a severe test in a Washington restaurant. She had lifted the olive from her martini and was saying to it "Little olive, forgive me, for I wrong you. But I too must be nourished and grow like the olive tree, to die and turn to compost nurturing future generations of your brothers and sisters. For are we not all part of the great cycle of life and death, giving and——" At this point, she said, two FBI agents arrested her and seized the olive, which they believed to contain a microphone. Thus gluttony, she finished, leads to all other deadly sins.

I was not convinced. How, for instance, could gluttony lead to anger? "Like this," she said, and struck me with her fist in the eye. "I am angry to you for not understanding nuttin'." My eye is still weeping, but at least the pain takes my mind off the tooth.

31 January

Dear Yam:

California here I am! And very depressed. Depression, at least, is not a deadly sin. Once again the movie on the plane was *Snow White*, and this time I had a chance to probe the childish film for deeper meanings. I now feel the Seven Dwarfs represent the Seven Deadly Sins:

Dopey (who swallows a bar of soap) is Gluttony.
Sneezy is Avarice (nothing to sneeze at, they say of money).
Bashful is Lust.
Doc (the bossy one) is Pride.
Grumpy is Anger.

Happy is Envy.
Sleepy is Sloth.

Now it is true that collectively the dwarfs typify all the sins (they all dig for precious jewels, lust after Snow, hate the wicked queen, etc) but the above table seems stronger; I have written it in its original (i.e., Assyrian) order, where it corresponds to the seven planets and seven heavens. The soul was said to leave the body at death, and ascend through these seven heavens in turn, giving up to each one aspect of its worldly frailty: To the Moon it gave gluttony; to Mercury, avarice; to Venus, lust; to the Sun, pride; to Mars, anger; to Jupiter, envy; and finally to Saturn, sloth. Finally it would ascend into the eighth, Empyrean, heaven, naked and purified, to become a star. 7-Up probably refers to this ascent, as the seven days of the week refer to these planets.

On the return journey, the soul descending to be born into a new person takes up these same burdens, but not in equal measure. Evidently the position of each planet determines just how much Venerean lust or Martian anger the soul gets, and so to know a man's character it is necessary to know his planet positions at birth. This is called *astrology*, and the Assyrians used it for everything. If, say, Sennacharib found that Mercury was doing such-and-such, he knew he would be getting an important letter at the end of the week; Venus spelled good news for any romantic interest; Mars a domestic tiff.

No wonder I'm depressed. Thus I see all about me the human intellect, that splendid dusky queen, o'erburdened with cuprous chains and carried to a desert shore, there to slave for gross King Stupidity, he of the visage graven in stones of loutish . . . Sorry, I seem unable to handle these earthstyle metaphors, especially with my tooth, my eye, and yes I can chronicle another injury. I offered a cigarette to the man next to me on the plane and he said, "No thank you! And I hope you won't smoke either!" And slammed the tiny metal ashtray so violently that it removed the tip of my little finger. I did not complain, so he did not apologize.

Curiously, he seemed to feel the accident had somehow won

my confidence, for he began telling me the story of his life, which he kept calling an economic miracle. I began to doze.

"Greed, avarice, cupidity, call it what you will, it ruled my life until I saw . . . Keynes could not work because all his supply and demand curves were really linked to money, based on metal, of which the supply is strictly . . . easy to contract the market, just use . . . short half-life like Hahnium, every so many nanoseconds it's twice as precious . . . infinitely contracted specie could only expand, I tried imaginary metal, half-life 0, call it Nullium . . . hypothetically an endless boom, but . . . back to nothing, see? Get it?"

I nodded.

"So starting at the other end we peg wages and prices to one another, let the old spiral go . . . but suppose value of Nullium itself pegged to cost-of-living index . . . infinite regress . . . nested equations . . . no more poverty, because everybody has all the real wealth he wants, based on this." He opened a small suitcase. "Here I have all the real wealth in the world." It was empty.

1 February

Dear Yam:

Today I visited the sunken city of Los Angeles, then the Hollywood Museum where by mistake I shook hands with a waxwork of Ed ("Kookie") Byrne. The teeth of his metal comb punctured my palm. Everybody else too busy, telling me how tacky and superficial Hollywood was in its heyday, to notice. The hand began to throb later on, when I was playing *golf* with some ex-president (*golf* is a game like *sham* except you get to use sticks to make it easier). He doddered like Pope Clyde, kept telling me he was not a crook, not a crook.

Guilt hangs over this planet like an udder over the skeleton of a calf, is that one okay? On to Chicago, where I have an appointment with a dentist.

3 February

Dear Yam:

Yesterday was my first chance to meet a few ordinary citizens of this planet. Dr Hrthe, the dentist, was busy with another patient when I arrived. I took a *chair* (something like a *wev*, only you bend the other way) and leafed through a few old copies of *Tooth Design*. Evidently Dr Hrthe shares a waiting room with a psycho-analyst, a Dr Selbstmorder, for I could clearly overhear a conversation from an adjoining office.

"Do I lie down on the couch or . . .?"

"If you like, Mr Psoas. May I call you Ira?"

Silence. Ira Psoas, the psychic tax lawyer! Surely not still alive—but no, of course it was his son.

"Very hard to begin, do I begin with my childhood or what?"

"If you like, Ira."

"Sure, sure. You know the reason I came to you, I thought you of all ha ha people could ha ha help me with my special problem. . . ."

"I'm here to help you, Ira. Shoot."

"God it's gonna sound stupid, silly . . . Okay, here goes."

Silence. I found a non-dental magazine on the coffee table, *Computer Life*. Someone had been through its pages, underlining words in no apparent pattern.

"I guess it all started when I was a kid, Dad gave me this pocket calculator, you know? I really liked it, I mean I had fun just multiplying two times two, stuff like that. I mean calculations gave me a kinda special feeling, you know?"

"I'd like to hear more about that special feeling, Ira."

"Okay, okay a hard-on. I was ten-years-old, I didn't hardly know—okay, maybe I did know, but it didn't seem wrong, not really. I mean I kept the thing in my pants pocket, just liked to work out a few things in secret now and then . . . I used to pretend like it was the real thing, a computer.

"See Dad told me I'd go blind and lose strength with all these calculations, but I just didn't care. Even when I played baseball, I always had to stop and figure my batting average . . . pretty soon I just stopped playing games, you know?"

"Go on, Ira."

"Well then when I was fifteen I started hanging around the crummy part of town, and I met this, like this older computer, she'd been through a lot of programs, stuff I'd never dreamed of. We played around a few times, nothing serious . . . I forgot all about her when I got to college, there was this freshman registration computer, you know, really big, dumb but big, I couldn't keep my hands off her. I guess you can figure out the rest: I got her in trouble and it cost a lot to have her fixed, the Dean called me into his office and told me I was disgusting, and they expelled me. That's when the headaches started."

"Go on."

"Well Dad sent me to this behavioral therapist, you know? To cure me. He'd show me a picture of an IBM 360, say, or hand me a punched card, and at the same time give me this electric shock. It seemed to work fine, you know? I straightened out, got a job cleaning cribbage boards, married a real nice girl. We got three kids now, wanna see their pictures?"

"If you like, Ira."

I saw the door was open just a crack, and I pushed it open further and looked in. Ira was even shorter than his father (who, I recalled from the banquet, was less than a foot tall). I could not see the pictures he was passing over the desk, only that they were perforated.

"Okay, so things were going swell, only one day after work I'm passing this computer-dating agency and something just—snaps. All of a sudden I need an electric shock real bad, my hands are shaking so much I can't hardly fill out the form. I can see this computer sitting there, waiting—and when the girl takes my form and goes out of the room for a second, boy I'm all over that machine."

"How did that make you feel, Ira?"

"Good at first and then—disgusted. Couldn't wait to pay my money and get out of there. Even so, I know I'll be back. It gets worse, next thing you know I've left my wife and kids and moved down to the Village. I'm living with this computer who does horoscopes. I'm living *off* her. I don't care any more, sure, she does it for anybody for a coupla bucks, you think I care?"

"How did that make you feel?"

"That's when I really started to flip-flop, I mean I got into heavy stuff, flashing displays, ALGOL——"

"Tell me more about ALGOL, Ira."

"Well it's short for algolagnia, that means sado-masochism, like electric shocks and all. Before I know it I'm walking past the IBM showroom and opening my overcoat, you know? And I'm calling up computers on the phone and talking dirty. I finally got busted, flashing in front of the IBM showroom. In front of them fancy hoity-toity machines, think they're too good for it, but let me tell you, they all want it, they're all begging for it . . . *Underneath, every computer is the same.*"

Silence. I began to wonder what was keeping Dr Hrthe.

Ira said, "I blame society. I mean I been set up for this, right? Everywhere you look, computers, even the gas bill, showing everything they got. And you ever notice these electronics stores, always on the same streets where they got porno movies and sex stores, dirty books and massage . . . Hell, computers know what the score is, I blame society with its binary standard, you know?"

"Sorry, Ira, our time's up."

In a moment the little patient came into the waiting room, sniffling. I held up the magazine. "Is this yours?"

"Yeah—no! I never seen it before!" He leapt for the door handle and rushed out. I looked through the magazine again, trying to make sense of its underlined words:

Rockwell
RAM
Fairchild
Texas Instruments (doubly underlined)
bit
flip-flop
gang punch
byte
magnetic core
IBM
Machines Bull
software
turnaround time
input device

Polymorphic Systems
entry point
Honeywell

"Next!" Dr Hrthe appeared, brandishing a pair of scissors and a comb. He explained that he'd be leaving all the detailed dental work to his robot assistant, but (so as not to waste the hydraulic chair) he'd be glad to give me a haircut.

"Now open wide," he said when I was in the chair, "and should I lower the part a little to cover that bald spot?"

I asked him about Dr Selbstmorder, and he laughed. "Him? He's nothing but a cheap robot headshrinker; you put a quarter in the slot and he listens to you for ten minutes. Real cheap, too, he's got about a dozen phrases he just keeps recycling: *Go on*, he says, and *How do you feel about that?* Not like my boy here, he's a fully-trained DDS, aren't you, boy?"

He was evidently addressing the dental chair itself, which seemed to manipulate its own instruments. After giving me a painful injection in the right eyeball, it brought a TV camera up to my mouth. "Terrible," it said. "These molars are going to give you a lot of trouble unless you start taking better care of them."

"About halfway down the ear?" Hrthe asked. "Yeah, Selbstmorder's a slob, never even gets up from behind his desk to shake hands with a patient. Course he can't, he's got no legs, nothing from the waist down but a pedestal. Like a counter-stool. Takes no pride in his work. No wonder the company that made him went out of business."

My eyeball hurt terribly. "Pride?" I asked, through a mouthful of machinery. "Isn't that a sin?"

"A rinse? You should have said so before I started." He hummed tunelessly and clacked his scissors. "Now me, I got pride in my work. You wouldn't think to look at me, that I was a clone, would you?"

I made a sound.

"Sure. Here, I got a family portrait." He showed me what looked like a battalion photo, tiers of identical men squinting at the sun (the planet associated with pride, I recalled). "247 of us, all dentists and barbers. Of course a lot of the boys are dead now, they joined this crazy religion that believes in suicide. The I WAS movement, very big stuff a few years back, every now and then they'd get together and drink cyanide mixed in Kool-Aid. Always thanking Jesus for taking away another day of their lives.

"Not as if they believed in an after-life, neither. They just liked being miserable, I guess, and death seemed the grand prize. They used to have a slogan, *It's good to feel bad.* So they went around humbling themselves, you know: trying to get short-changed in stores, asking friends to tell them shaggy dog stories, eating Big Macs, going again and again to *The Sound of Music*, voting for Ronald Reagan . . . real dreamers."

The injection was taking effect; I became a dreamer myself. It seemed to me I was in a war room with General Stulm, in the middle of a terrible war—which he kept calling a game. He rolled the dice and moved some battalions, the 7th Deathray and the 777th Plague.

"Seven come eleven," he muttered. "Beat that!"

Looking closer I noticed that one of the tiny men on the board was Ira Psoas, another was Grumpy. They were playing with miniature dice on an even smaller board, where a group of plague viruses stood waiting to move, while their own leaders shook small molecules and rolled a seven. Suddenly some giant unseen hand gave our war-room a tremendous shove, and the doors burst open. Ed Byrne clones poured in through every exit, raking the room with comb-fire. I was hit in the eyeball, and as I fell, I heard the General mutter, "Lucky bastard! Wonder what he threw?"

Suddenly the game began again, Yam, and you and I were the players. My first roll of the dice, a four, sank Hollywood, and my second, an eight, sank everything else. Just then a messenger ran in, drank Kool-Aid and died. I prised the slip of paper from his hand and read:

NOTRE HUD OK NO.
TO LOG TO'RDS RX LANK HE I HAD CZAR.
ADZES 8 OL' ON NO SNOB FIT MF.

OUR GHOST A MA: SNOB NOW NEEDY!

When I had decoded it, it made far more sense:

OPUS FIVE. PLOP.
UP MPH UPSET SYMBOL IF JIBE DABS.
BE AFT 9 PM POOP TOP *C. G. JUNG.*
PT SHIP (TUB) NB: TOP COPY OF FEZ!

When I came to, I was aching, sick and dizzy, and my hair was parted all wrong.

11 February

Dear Yam:

You didn't get my last letter because I didn't write one. I've been very busy, really tied up, also not too well. In fact—but let me begin where I left off:

I was supposed to go straight from the dentist to New York, where I would address the UN (United Nations) and appear on a TV talk show. But our plane was hijacked and one of my feet was shot off. I don't want to harp on my health problems, but it wasn't pleasant. I had to go into a hospital anyway, to clear up some minor infections of the hand, mouth, eye, other hand and scalp; while I was there they fitted me with an elegant artificial foot (it can do any dance step at all, which is more than I can say for my real foot). A psychiatrist came to see me, too, to ask if I felt alienated. I told him it was only what I expected, being an alien, and he got angry and left. But he sent me an enormous bill, and so did the hospital, the surgeon, the prosthetic foot company, the laboratory, drug companies, the anaesthetist, Dr Hrthe, and so on. On top of it all, the TV show sued me for non-appearance. I was broke and desperate and not even allowed to leave the hospital. I just had to lie there day after day, watching TV game shows and soap operas.

There was one intriguing program—not sure if it was a game show or a soap opera—called *Beggar Thy Neighbor.* It involved five couples, the Joneses, Smiths, Blacks, Greens and Hydes, and their possessions:

Mrs Green's infra-red hairdrier was as inferior to the

microwave hairdrier of Mrs Hyde, as the latter's thermodynamic washing detergent system was to the former's (geoprophylactic) system. That gives you an idea of the ground rules, and they fought it out for weeks with 883-program sewing machines, electric-eye cat doors, rotary-engine personal transit systems, electric spoons and laser toasters. A hologram recorder beat a nuclear-powered artificial heart, and both beat an ultrasonic dishwasher or an auto-rotisserie with Magic-Nose trace element analyser.

For a while the Joneses bluffed with their old digital clock radio that roasts and grinds coffee, and their laser room divider turned out to be fake. Mr Smith weighed in with his auto-bowling critic, his sonar fishing rod and his programmable pizza chef, and the real fight was on. Electric nail-buffers with cuticle attachments, kit-built windmills, solar-triggered flag-poles, electrostatic coffee filters, heat pumps, digital urine testers and calorimeters, electric swizzle sticks, a shopper-chef kitchen system, a luminosity monitor to help avoid eyestrain, a hexaphonic sound center, and an electronic organ with lost chord finder. And much, as they say, much more.

The winners got a big pile of new stuff, cars, furs, jewelry, canasta decks, free trips to Southern Macauleyland, screen tests at the Hollywood Museum, dinner with a baseball team, free tax advice and a superb home to keep it all in, complete with an advanced security system. The losers had to bring all their stuff to the studio and see it smashed up by a gang of black kids who looked hungry. Wonderful stuff.

Anyway, there I was wondering (still) how you could really define the seven deadly sins, also wondering how to get out of the hospital, when all my problems were solved at once.

Mr Polk, president of Polk Leisure Industries, came to visit me with a special offer. PLI had designed a new Total Leisure system, and was now trying to sign up celebrities to test and testify. He already had General Stulm (now retiring), Madame Late, Ira Psoas and a few others, but what better testimonial could PLI get than mine? If an extra-terrestrial alien was happy with the gadget, who could resist it? If I agreed, therefore, PLI would pay all my bills, and of course pay for "installation".

I was at first wary. Installation involved major surgery, indeed a total body transplant of sorts. The individual is reduced to a few key brain cells, which are installed in the Total Leisure Center permanently. From then on, he guaranteed, boredom is impossible. One may watch all TV channels at the same time, while playing a (simulated) round of golf, set of tennis, rubber of bridge and so on. One may climb Everest by every known route at once, while at the same time winning the Gillette Cup and walking on the Moon. One can browse among the entire contents of great libraries, art galleries; attend concerts, and of course write, paint and compose; witness scientific discoveries or make them; shoot it out with dangerous criminals or dangerous cops; even die and come back to enjoy it. Any human activity that can be recorded on PLI cassettes, he explained, is yours. I took a chance and signed up. The operation is tomorrow; this may be my last letter.

18 February

Dear Yam:

This is my last letter. The operation took seven hours, and I felt my soul giving up all its gluttony to the Moon, all its avarice to Mercury, all its lust to Venus, and so on. It was not until I lost the capacity for these sins that I finally understood them. Everything since is an anticlimax. TV seems full of re-runs, once you've won the Gillette Cup or made nine holes-in-one in succession, it loses something. The arts are not so hot, either: paint-by-numbers, Grandma Moses, Reader's Digest Condensed Books—the tastes of my old friend Rep (who invented this gadget) prevail. I climbed Everest the other day, only to find a sign (done with a paint-by-numbers set): HO HU. Evidently the sign-writer was overcome by lethargy before he could finish.

I thought of finishing it for him. But why bother? Let the next dwarf take over.

AFTERWORD

One of my own favorites. The theme of seven deadly sins was suggested by Emma Tennant, who commissioned this for her anthology called The Saturday Night Reader.

Like "Guesting", this concerns an alien visitor, but it is meant to be almost the mirror reflection of that story. In "Guesting" the alien is absorbed by, used and discarded by the media. Here it is the alien who attempts to absorb and assimilate notions of good and evil.

We tend to forget how parochial our notions of good and evil are. Outside Western cultures, our species seems less concerned with sin and guilt than with questions of practicality and propriety. Easterners may be concerned with being respectable, with seeking the absence of desire or with keeping to their station in life, but they are seldom overwhelmed by guilt.

Only our own odd corner of the species seems to have evolved these complex, curious notions of good and evil so pervasive and so binding that almost everyone who doesn't wander around feeling guilty about everything (from overeating to not joining CND) is probably in a state of mortal sin. Those who do feel guilty are of course guilty too: to the ten commandments we have added Joseph Heller's wonderful invention, Catch-22.

I was raised a Roman Catholic, and so received my pile of guilt early on in life. From the age of seven I went around feeling uneasy about all the sins I must have committed, but couldn't remember in the confessional. Confession only made things worse: it was considered pious to confess regularly, but unless you had a lot of sins to confess so that you needed regular confession, what was the point? You couldn't invent sins or imagine guilt, either, because that was having a "scrupulous conscience"—a sin in itself. And if the whole insoluble problem made you despair, well, that *was a sin too. There were Catches-22, 23 and so on, right on to Catch-Infinity.*

So it seemed until, when I was twelve, the Catholic school I attended made the mistake of teaching me apologetics. Up to this time, the religious arrangements of the universe had been taken for granted, like gravity or water. Now we were told that you could prove God's existence in four (count 'em) ways!

It took no time at all for me to realize that if you could prove God's existence, it was a matter for disputation, not a fact. I decided that either I was all wrong, or else the notion of a God who wanted me to feel guilty was all wrong. I struggled out of my bonds, leapt to the window, and with one bound I was free.

An Explanation for the Disappearance of the Moon

My labors come to an end. The death of the system must finally come to each part of the system, even to my part. I know that outside my windows, opaque with grime, the social order—or what we mistook for the social order—is gently sinking into silence. Perhaps no one will notice. Or perhaps a solitary woman, pushing a pram across the flat green rectangle of the park, will pause a moment and listen: Is her child crying? Breathing? There will be no sound bar the last few ticks of her own heart. When that too fails, she will sink to the earth, and within her the blood will sink to the underside of her body.

It may seem odd that I still consider myself part of the system. I am, after all, divorced, jobless, penniless, insane and a murderer. But let us set aside such relative terms and deal in absolutes.

The Moon. Anagrams include *mono, no om*. Or call it Luna, anagrams include *anul*. It all began with just such trivial wordplay, which led me to check the etymology of the word *moon*. OED traces it to Old Teutonic, where it plausibly meant "to measure". Skeat believes it can be traced to the Sanskrit *ma*, "to measure", which also means to think, to compare, to diminish or to cut down. But then Skeat traces everything to Sanskrit; probably because his own name resembles "Sanskrit" cut down and diminished. In truth, no one knows where MOON came from. A heavy word, for an object supposedly light enough to float in the sky.

The letters of *moon* float, disconnected: a double cusp, two circles, a single cusp. Thus they floated before my eyes one day, when (making an effort to shut out the sound of one of my children wailing) I realized: *moon* is one of the few English words which may be entirely written in Ogham script, that curious syllabary of the ancient Celts:

moon

Ogham is named after the Celtic god Ogmios, whom the Romans confused with their own Hercules. Lucian reported being shown a picture of Ogmios as an old man clad in a lion's skin and leading a group of followers by delicate chains of gold and amber attached to his tongue. The followers did not regret their loss of liberty, he was told, but heaped praises upon their captor. This, Lucian found, represented eloquence, a gift more powerful than physical strength.

Ogham is written in tongue-shaped symbols. According to the fourteenth century *Book of Ballymote*, they were used to inscribe "The Wand of the Poet". These Celts worshipped the moon as a goddess called Arianrhod ("silver wheel").

My research went no further until (shortly after losing all the money I had invested in an electric car firm) I dreamed that I was reading a book entitled *The Moon and Sixpence*. Imagine my astonishment to awaken and find that there really was such a book! Silver again: I began to wonder whether W. Somerset Maugham were not a Celtic poet.

Turning to a genuine Celtic poet, W. B. Yeats, I found two references to the Moon, each mentioning silver:

to carry the sun in a golden cup, and the Moon in a silver bag

and

the silver apples of the Moon

I now saw there must be some deep, enigmatic connection between the Moon, Celts and money. And perhaps music:

I found that the composer Edward Elgar in 1897 wrote a cipher message, using Ogham symbols. He sent this message to his friend, Dora *Penny*. It was never deciphered. Nor was Elgar's musical Enigma, the secret of his *Enigma Variations*. I noticed that the word "enigma" somewhat resembled the Celtic "Ogmios".

At this point, other matters intervened to put the entire problem out of my mind temporarily. My youngest child smothered in her cot (the oldest had already been killed, I forgot to mention, by an experimental model of an electric car, during its only test run). Subsequent deep depression caused my wife to resort to tranquillizers. In an effort to cheer her up, I purchased a range of household appliances which we could ill afford. These evidently overloaded the wiring in our old house, causing a fire. My wife threw our remaining child out the window to a passing stranger; the boy has not been seen since. I was forced to stay home from the office for a few days to care for my wife after her suicide attempt. In consequence, I lost my job, just as she entered an expensive course of psychoanalysis. It was not until I'd cashed in the equity on my life insurance and taken out a second mortgage that I was once more free to investigate the Moon.

I decided to put aside Elgar and Ogham for the moment, and instead decipher Yeats's enigmatic lines. Why should the sun be carried in a cup, the Moon in a bag? Cups may be used for objects subject to gravity, but in free-fall, bags must be used. Then was gravity involved? Gravity reminded me of Newton, and his apple. "The silver apples of the Moon"—yes! Now I was getting somewhere:

Every apple reference I could think of seemed to involve gravity. Newton watched his fictitious apple fall, it is said, and deduced that the earth rose to meet it. The force of attraction between any two objects is directly proportional to their masses, and inversely proportional to the square of the distance between their centres. Yet the Moon rises.

Apples in literature invoke gravity: The apple of discord was *thrown down* into an assembly of the gods, who immediately *fell* into an argument over it. Likewise the William Tell story involves accurate archery: computing in advance the parabolic trajectory of an arrow moving under the influence of gravity. Other references are numerous and obvious. We are cautioned not to "upset the apple cart". Love apples are associated with *falling* in love. In Eden an apple caused the Fall of Man.

The message was clear: If I could somehow destroy the gravity-apple of Isaac Newton, the universe could yet be saved. Does that sound arrogant? But science tells us that it is gravity which is destroying our universe, and gravity alone. Black holes, blacker than eclipses of the Moon, are——

At this point, work was again interrupted, when my wife deserted me. I felt suddenly under the deadly assault of gravity waves. Even eating and sleeping were too difficult. I could only sit in a chair staring at the television—until that too was taken away. The burnt-out shell of the house began to resemble a black hole. I learned all about black holes from television. These are spots of gravity so intense that nothing can escape from them, not even light. (One sees the dead hand of Newton here again, for aside from gravity, he dabbled in optics.) Inside a black hole, light is bent so severely that it forms a circle. According to the mathematician John Taylor, one might stand within a black hole and get a perfect view of the back of one's own head. Black holes are, he maintains, a sign that the universe is running down like a great clock. (As a boy, Newton built a wooden clock.) Eventually everything will sink into black holes and vanish. They are full stops to all. If a full stop black hole should come near the Moon, it would suck the Moon into oblivion.

That is not the explanation.

Resuming work, I saw that Newton's law depends upon the understanding that planets move in elliptical orbits. This presupposes that there is such a figure as an ellipse. I resolved to demonstrate that there are no ellipses.

Proof No. 1: That there are no ellipses.

1. Ellipses are elongated circles.
2. There are no circles.
3. Therefore there are no elongated circles.
4. Therefore there are no ellipses.

This seemed a sound, tight proof, but for step (2). Could I prove the non-existence of circles? While I was in hospital having some ECT, the house was repossessed. I moved into a furnished room on the top floor of a squat. There I showed that there are no circles.

Proof No. 2: That there are no circles.

1. It is impossible to "square the circle", i.e., to construct a square with the same area as a given circle, using only compasses and straight-edge. To do so would involve constructing a length *pi*, which cannot be done.
2. For the same reasons, it is impossible to "triangle" the circle or "pentagon" the circle, or construct a figure of any

number of sides, n, equal in area to a given circle.

3. It is also impossible to construct a figure of 0 sides.
4. From number theory: Whatever is true of the number 0, and when true of some number n also true of $n + 1$, is true of all numbers.
5. Therefore no figure of any number of sides can be constructed equal to a given circle.
6. A circle is itself a polygon of an infinite number of sides (and infinity is a number).
7. Therefore a circle cannot be copied by another circle; all circles must be of different sizes.
8. In this figure, a big circle contains two small ones, which meet at its center. But (by 7) they cannot be the same size.

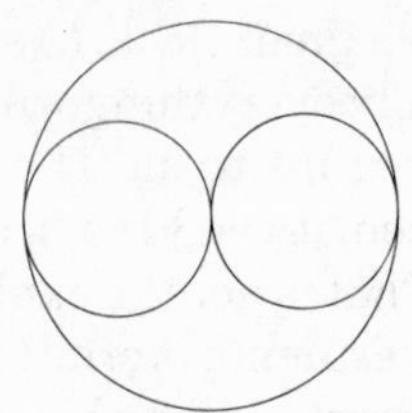

9. Therefore the centre of the big circle is not in its centre, or in other words, it is not a circle.
10. Since the same figure can be drawn for every circle, there are no true circles.

I had reached a critical stage in my work, and now I feared the forces of Newtonism would close in to prevent my finishing. I now knew there is no law of gravity. Indeed, the Earth is trying to push us away, and we, by some biological perversity, have learned how to counter this force and sink Earthwards.

I learned that levitating persons were common enough in the past, before Newton. The last authenticated case was the celebrated "flying monk", Joseph Copertino, who flew in front of hundreds of witnesses. Leibniz travelled to Apulia to see him fly. Copertino went on flying all his life, and even made a last, feeble levitation from his death-bed, on 18th September, 1663. That was the exact day when Newton, at Cambridge, commenced his infamous calculations. Man, he declared, would fly no more. Light itself will be trapped in black holes, for people to see the backs of their own heads.

The little man claimed to be reading the meter. But as he came in the room I felt the sickening surge of gravity waves. I waited until he bent down to shine his light on something under the sink, and then I picked up a set of bathroom scales and smashed in the back of his head. The gravity waves stopped at once.

Man would fly no more, declared Newton. Man would see no more. His optical laws were to put out our eyes, as his gravity nailed us to the ground.

The contradistinctions *light/dark* and *light/heavy* had always seemed accidents of language. Yet we know that persons who attained divine ecstasies not only flew into the air, but glowed with inner light. And now physicists tell us light too is subject to gravity: "brightness falls from the air" as solid apples bend beams of light.

Newton contributed to optics the notion that white light is made up of exactly seven colors of the rainbow, no more, no less. Yet we are told that the ancients saw no such colors. Aristotle and Xenophanes thought the rainbow was purple, red and yellow only. Democritus knew only the colors red, yellow, black and white. Homer thought the sea was the same color as wine. Green and blue, evidently, are recent inventions, derived by Newton from the prismatic bending of light. He bent light as gravity bends it, in an effort to destroy.

My bathroom scales no longer work. If my experiment works, no one will ever need scales again. The scales will fall from their eyes. The pennies will drop.

The Moon might be a coin that someone snatches from the sky and drops into a meter. That is not the explanation. Celtic coins were copied from Greek and Roman coins. But, not knowing what they were copying, the Celtic coiners turned the sober features of gods and emperors into strange, beautiful abstract designs: explosions of circles, dots, curves and curls.

The police come to the door to ask about the meter reader, who has been missing since Monday. They could look over my shoulder and see the man's corpse, but perhaps there are in my room peculiar optical laws unknown to Newton. They are only slightly suspicious when I look at my watch and ask them to leave. I go to the window, open it and look up and, for a moment, wonder if all my work has been in vain. The eclipse is not taking place.

Then it begins: the merest shadow of fuzziness at one edge of a perfectly circular disc. My experiment will guarantee this eclipse's permanence. The end of the Moon will mean the end of human madness and strife. One day, Man will be able to see a thousand colors that do not exist for us. He will be able to see the front of his own head!

The police begin banging at the door, behind me. "We know you're in there."

They know nothing. I am a black hole of obscurity, a flying mirror of darkness. The fear that has held us all prisoner on Newton's Earth no longer binds me.

When I step out, unafraid, I will only appear to fall. In reality, I will cause a genuine levitation of the entire world.

Afterword

This story has had several lives. The first version, written in the late 1960s, was lost by my agent of the time, who also managed to lose the only carbon copy. I had entrusted the top copy to their American branch, and the carbon to their British branch, in the foolish belief that it would be impossible for both to vanish. I rewrote it twice, but I never could get over the feeling that the original had something I could never quite recapture.

Partly what can't be reproduced is the feel *of writing a new story. There is some point in the writing of any story when I know it's right, when it begins to unfold almost automatically and discover itself to me. It's a kind of* Aha! *reaction, as Koestler would have said, and much the same sort of exhilaration I get from seeing the point of a joke or the answer to a problem. There's nothing like it, and I suspect it's why I write, if not why every writer writes. I notice that Ray Bradbury says he writes every story in one sitting, in one day. So do I and so do others I've talked to about it. The fever seems to last for a limited amount of time, and for each story, it happens only once.*

How to Make Major Scientific Discoveries at Home in Your Spare Time

When I was a kid, I could never decide whether I wanted to grow up to be a Nobel Prize-winning scientist or a Yellow Cab. My early interest in science was stimulated by the gift of a kaleidoscope for my fourth birthday. I turned it to the sky and immediately discovered eight new moons of Jupiter. Unfortunately, no one believed me until it was too late. By the time I managed to persuade a grown-up to verify my discovery, these moons had all disintegrated or else been repossessed. There was nothing left to see but a few fragments of what looked like ordinary colored glass.

So disheartening was this experience that I nearly gave up science. I smashed the kaleidoscope, and many years were to pass before I could bring myself to look through another. (Yet only last year, using an electron kaleidoscope of my own invention, I isolated the virus which causes people to join the American Legion.)

My grandmother also tried to discourage me from full-time science. One morning at breakfast—she always had a raw egg, sipped straight from the shell through a small hole—she said, "Forget science. Nobody ever made a living out of it."

"Nobody, Granny?"

"I read it the other day, how all these scientists admit they still can't make a living in a test tube. Or was it life they couldn't make? Whatever it is, they all admit it."

I never forgot her words. Out of gratitude, I told her how to make a second small hole in the other end of the egg, to make the sucking easier. Meanwhile I gave up science as a career and went into the family business, retail snoods. Before long I was able to expand the firm, diversifying into retail geography.

Yet my heart remained in the laboratory, as they say in the transplant-leaseback racket. I spent all my spare time reading science texts and mixing up chemicals to see what color came out. I began wrestling with significant, fundamental questions about our universe: Does ontogeny *really* recapitulate phylogeny? Why is the sky blue? Do giraffes ever get sore throats? This old universe of ours didn't always give me the answers. But now and then—with a little persistence and a whole lot of luck—I managed to come up with a major scientific breakthrough. For example:

Solar energy. Those who hope for cheap energy from the sun are wasting their time. As I showed in 1962, *the sun isn't really hot at all*. Its surface temperature is no more than forty degrees in the shade, and there is hardly any shade. The sun only seems hot to us because the light coming from it has to rub against our atmosphere, which warms it up. Space shuttles have the same problem on re-entry.

This phenomenon also explains the seasons. In winter, since the air is colder, sunlight is colder too. This leads to a cooling of the earth that we know as winter. Summer likewise only occurs in warm weather.

The reason this sensational discovery hasn't been reported in the press earlier is that the US and USSR are secretly engaged in an all-out race to the sun. Whoever plants the first flag on the sun could claim the entire solar system, excluding one or two neighborhoods in Chicago.

Mathematics. In 1974 I developed an improved value for the ratio *pi*. Mathematicians have been troubled by this unruly number for centuries. Back in 1453, when an international congress met to decide on a world-wide standardized wheel of *circular* shape, Leonardo Da Vinci warned them about *pi*. *Pi* never comes out even, no matter how many decimal places of it you calculate. To this day, valuable computer time is wasted in carrying out *pi* to millions of places, every time anybody wants to draw a circle.

My improved value of *pi* does away with all this waste. I'm not allowed to publish the new value—it is of course classified—but here's a hint: From now on, all circles are going to be a whole lot rounder.

Archaeology. In 1977, during a Mesopotamian dig, I ran across the lost thirteenth sign of the zodiac. The re-emergence of this ancient sign promised to explain much about astrology, for instance why it doesn't work very well. The reason was obvious: for millennia both layman and adept had been relying on a completely false twelve-sign zodiac. It would now be possible to make all horoscopes 100% accurate. A newspaper might say: "Your moodiness will pass. Monday's a good day for gardening, unless that romantic attachment at the office seems promising. Avoid squid, and ignore the advice of a friend at your peril. A letter late in the week could bring big news or stamps on approval."

This could now be reinterpreted as: "Advise your friend at the office to eat squid on Monday. You will pass out at a garden party, but a letter will bring you an inheritance of $4,323,864.14 after tax."

I brought the resurrected sign with me to Venice, to have it cleaned. But when I left it on the window sill to dry, a careless chambermaid knocked it off into the Grand Canal. It has never been retrieved.

Exploration. In 1969 I headed an expedition to look for the East Pole, and a long, hard struggle it was. Most of the party were lost at base camp, due to problems with the tents. Base camp was located on the Indian Ocean, and pitching tents on water turned out to be difficult and dangerous. I alone managed to reach the Pole and sink a flag. The expedition took my entire summer vacation.

Next year, when we try for the West Pole, we hope to be better equipped: tents held down by anchors instead of stakes, buoyant dogsleds, and Huskies which are good swimmers.

Quark medicine. Until recently, most people probably found the field of particle physics kind of remote and esoteric. Some folks don't know a baryon from a hadron, a meson from a lepton. They can't name the three kinds of neutrino or the five kinds of quark, the eight gluons or any of the anti-particles, either. But now a new medical breakthrough of mine makes all *important to anyone concerned about the health of ody's atomic nuclei.*

he story began with a correspondence course on the particles: proton, neutron, electron. It wasn't easy. All too often the sample particles the school sent me got lost. Once I was sent an envelope with a tiny hole in it—the tiny electrons had all leaked out in the mails. Once instead of neutrons the school (which also ran courses in animal husbandry) sent me a nutria which ate all my notes.

I persevered, however, studying other particles and their different properties: mass, energy, spin and charge. Quarks have two more properties besides: *color* and *charm*.

Color and charm! The properties most highly prized in cosmetic work! If mere lasers (color and energy) could be used to remove birthmarks, what could be done with more sophisticated particles? I devoted all my spare time for the past two years to the project. Today, of course, my patented *quark ray* is used in beauty clinics the world over—wherever people need to remove unwanted facial positrons.

Philosophy. It hasn't all been pure research. I've also spent my spare time on larger questions. Long before C.P. Snow, I was the first one to point out that there are two cultures that never communicate with each other. "Snowy" probably heard of my idea and repeated it, but he got it wrong. He claimed the two cultures were science and the liberal arts. But I was talking about two other cultures entirely. One is the culture of a South American tribe called the wow !. The ! are incredibly shy, and though they possess a rich language, both oral and written, they never use it. In fact, no one has ever seen or heard them.

The other culture is a yeast culture in a brewery in Budapest, which shows no sign of wanting to communicate with the ! or anyone else. These two cultures have very little in common. They don't belong to the same species, they live in different places, and they haven't been introduced.

Evolution. My current research is approaching another breakthrough that will resolve the great evolution vs. creationism debate. Essentially the two arguments run as follows: Creationists argue that man could not evolve from the ape because (1) Man, unlike the ape, has six fingers on each hand and can wiggle his ears; (2) Noah's Ark was 300 cubits long, 50 wide and 30 high (unlike primate arks); and (3) There are no apes anyway. The so-called apes in zoos are only men dressed up in hairy suits.

Evolutionists, on the other hand, argue that giraffes got their long necks because generation after generation of giraffes stretched up to eat the leaves on trees and the taller ones got more leaves. There are two things wrong with this argument: (1) Giraffes didn't need to stretch, since they had very long necks; (2) What about dolphins? They live in the ocean *where there are no trees.*

Now my new line of research seems to show that there is some truth in both sides of the argument. Preliminary tests suggest that man evolved from furniture—whether from ladderback chairs or horsehair chesterfields we don't yet know. Nor have hassocks or end tables been eliminated yet, I'm sorry to say. The picture is so far not clear, and it may turn out that furniture evolved from people. Noah's Ark, we now believe, was filled with second-hand coffee tables, bridge lamps and formica dinette sets, and the Deluge itself was a kind of grand clearance sale.

Much remains to be done here, if I can spare the spare time from my bioengineering and cybernetic hobbies, and my plan to dig to China.

AFTERWORD

Once I worked as a technical writer, explaining how to take apart things like fork-lift trucks and put them back together. The experience gave me a lasting appreciation of all good explanations. You've no idea how hard it is to tell someone how to perform any simple task without making any mistakes. There are probably people today still puzzling over why their fork-lift trucks look all wrong when they get them back together.

I enjoy explaining things, however, and I enjoy having things explained to me. In Britain there are wonderful TV programs explaining everything imaginable. One of my favorites is Tom Keating, the famous forger of paintings, explaining just how to go about faking a Titian or a Degas.

Another is a program specifically aimed at the mentally handicapped, which explains how to do simple tasks like using a vacuum cleaner. I learned from it that you have to hold the cord in one hand to keep it out of the way. I'd never thought of this before. For years, I'd taken it for granted that you just went on tripping over the cord or getting it under the vacuum cleaner's wheels, that this was a fact of life. That program has given me a completely new perspective on the notion of mental handicap.

Okay, that's enough humility for now. Come on, you guys, the humility break is over. Back to work. We got us a frik loft truck to put together, and this time let's get it right.

The Kindly Ones

"Must be some sin," the patient whispered. "Must be I've committed . . . Barbara thought eating liver, maybe. Not that I've ever really liked liver . . . black coals or. . . ."

From time to time, in the normal diagram of all such consultations, the doctor would lean forward across his scarred oak desk and ask a sympathetic question. From what time to what time?

"I hated to come to you," the patient whispered, "with a little complaint like this."

"That's just what I'm here for, Mr Edhulme. And laryngitis isn't always such a 'little complaint'. Lots of flu going around these days. You may have picked up something. In any case, I know just the stuff." He wrote a prescription, tore it off the pad and offered it. "Two teaspoonfuls twice a day. If the throat doesn't clear up, come back and see me next week. All right?"

The doctor's behavior is theoretically predictable: the movement forward, head rigid and eyes on his watch, the timbre of his voice, the frame of reference of his next remark. Of course, with the crude statistical tools of that day (Wednesday, June 20th), no such refined analysis would be possible.

"Picked up something, yes." Edhulme made no move to go. Eleven thirty-two registered on the doctor's watch, which he had earlier removed and placed on the corner of his desk blotter. The chorus—

"Was there anything else, Mr Edhulme?"

"Well, it isn't just my throat trouble, doctor. There have been other little punishments. Going on for so long. Croak, grawp." Edhulme's whisper went on for so long, listing complaints: Popping of the ears, a bitten tongue, a slight backache. . . .

"But there's nothing else wrong right now, at this moment in time?" asked the doctor at eleven thirty-four.

Tears rolled about Edhulme's eyes as he shook his head (Sorry to say, I'm healthy as a horse). The doctor promised to give him a complete checkup sometime. At some future date.

> These people believe that when the spell has been written on the prescription pad, the devil will go away. (Writing is strong magic, an aid to memory.) In reality, it is the *patient* who goes away. The doctor tears off the page and makes him walk out with it, leaving himself the blank pad. He does not want to remember the patient or his devil. When the patient has gone, he washes his hands.
>
> Pendleton's *Western Magic*

A dirty day. Edhulme's discarded prescription blew away down the street, driven by the same gust that dropped a fleck of dried mud in his eye. If you have anything in your eye, don't rub it. Weeping helps.

Rubbing it, Edhulme rehearsed his next appointment: "Barbara thought maybe it was Martians, operating out of radioactive canals or something. She's not too bright about the universe. But take black holes. . . ."

"No, no, the throat's fine. Only now I have this. *This*." He opened his collar and peeled off a pink plastic patch to uncover a small boil.

"I see. Giving you a lot of pain, is it?"

Edhulme delivered his rehearsed sentence: "It isn't the pain so much as the punishment. I just don't like the way they're getting at me. For what? That's what I'd like to know, for what?"

The chorus—

"They?"

"The way I see it, they probably come from outer space. Something to do with those black holes I've been reading so much about lately."

"Black coals, I see."

"*Holes*. Doctor, do you believe there is intelligent life all over the universe?"

Thus rages the old controversy. The doctor might select his reply from any of the time-honored arguments disputed and refuted since the days of Origen—since the nights when man first looked into the sun and saw his own reflection. Is not life a Great Mystery? Define your terms. Is there intelligent life in this room? God does not play darts with the universe. Life is what you make it.

"Actually I don't know a great deal about astronomy," he said. "But what do you believe? Do you for instance believe that someone came from outer space to give you a small boil on the neck?"

"Well I know it sounds silly if you put it like that. All the same, these little punishments must mean something. Laryngitis. A nosebleed. Paper cuts. A slight toothache. Something in my eye for a whole day. One continual round of *torture.*"

The doctor doodled on his desk blotter. "Come now, isn't that putting it a bit strong? We all suffer little complaints from time to time. A paper cut is hardly red-hot iron tongs. It's just part of life. We can't all go round wrapped in cotton wool, can we?"

The chorus continued, while Edhulme thought over this suggestion. "I guess this just shows how clever they are. Using small things. If they broke my leg every week, you wouldn't dare think I was just a hypochondriac."

The doctor said something soothing. He was there to help all his patients, etc. He doodled a burning man, running, apparently pursued by a telephone number. "Tell me how you feel in general. Sleeping well?"

"Well enough, I suppose. Except when I had that ingrown toenail. I couldn't find a comfortable position where it wouldn't rub on the sheets."

"Yes, you came to see me about that."

"And as soon as it cleared up, I slept so soundly I got a stiff neck."

"Hmm. Eating normally, are you?"

"I choke on my food a lot. I usually get some caught between my teeth, as well. Yesterday I sneezed a cup of tea up my nose. It wasn't hot tea, though. Last month, I burned my tongue——"

"Yes, yes. Are you worried about anything, say, at work?"

Edhulme described his job as exciting, secret, dangerous

government scientific work. Mixing secret formulae in the interests of national defense.

"Really?"

No really he worked as a file clerk in a drawing office, for the local council. The copies of drawings which he filed had been developed by some ammonia process.

"The ammonia makes the paper cuts sting," he said. "I understand there may be forms of life in the universe that breathe nothing but pure ammonia—imagine that."

"Everything all right at home, then?"

Edhulme had been living with a cat, a budgie and a fiancée. The fiancée had left him. Who remained?

"Did these little 'punishments' start after Barbara left you? After you quarrelled?"

The patient told him all about the space creatures.

"We can't know what they're like, for sure. They live in black holes, out in space. You can't see into a black hole, it's so dark. Invisible, like. It doesn't exist. If you fell into a black hole, did you know that time would come to a complete stop?"

"Is that so?"

"Or maybe it's the other way around. The main thing about a black hole is, nothing can ever get out of it, ever. It's very deep. The only thing that can get out are these little particles. They send them to strike me."

"Particles."

"I call them *punishons*. One struck me here on the neck."

Listening to the chorus, the doctor framed another question: "Why do you suppose they would want to punish you?"

"I don't know. Maybe they want to kill me, but they can't. Or maybe this is all for my own good. They want to reform me. Reform the world. They want me to give up everything and everyone."

The doctor persuaded him to visit Dr Morphe, a psychiatrist. "Just stop and see my receptionist on the way out. She can telephone for an appointment." Over the intercom he told Doris to telephone for an appointment.

The chorus of coughs from the waiting room, which had paused for principal speeches, now resumed:

1st voice:	Or	Or	Or	Ora	Or	Ora	Or	Ora	Or	Or
2nd voice:	Ha	Ra-	a-	a-	a-	ark!				
3rd voice:	Emp		Emp	Emp		Emp	Emp		Emp	Emp
4th voice:		He			He-	Hume			He	
5th voice:			Ca-	hoot	Co-	hort		Ko-	hou-	tek-
6th voice:	ef		ef	ef		ef	ef	ef		ef

* * *

The man who limped in looked like a casualty from an animated cartoon: a great pear-shaped bandage on his thumb, a sling on the opposite arm, an oversized turban of surgical gauze, a plaster over the bridge of his nose—even a tiny flag of white toilet paper stuck to his chin by a Rising Sun drop of blood. The doctor recognized Edhulme at once.

"You can start by taking off all those home-made ornaments, starting with the sling. I don't suppose you've broken your arm?"

"Bumped my elbow." Edhulme showed the doctor his sprained thumb, the boil on his nose, the spot where he'd banged his head on the bathroom cabinet door.

"I was washing my hair—terrible dandruff attack—and soap went into my eyes. Still, that's better than the stye I had——"

"Why didn't you keep your appointment with Dr Morphe?"

"I woke up on the day with murderous cold sores and a sore tongue. I could hardly talk." The rest of the story vanished in a sneezing fit.

"If you won't seek help, Mr Edhulme, you'll just have to soldier on alone."

"Alone? Yes, that's what they've been trying to tell me. My cat scratches me now, and I've got an allergy to my budgie's feathers. The little punishons are making me give up everyone."

"They made you give up your girl? Your Barbara?"

"Well." Edhulme's ears blushed. "You see, I . . . it in my . . ."

"Sorry? I didn't catch that."

The blush spread, showing up a dozen tiny white razor nicks on the patient's cheeks. "I said I caught it in my trousers zip. Pinched it, the tenderest part. Well, *that* will never happen again, touch wood." He touched the desk.

"That's an interesting old custom," said the doctor. "I believe it came from the Druids, worshipping their tree gods. It was dangerous saying anything positive without propitiating them. Touching wood."

Edhulme looked at his finger, then sucked it.

"Splinter? Oh, I am sorry. This old desk . . ."

"It doesn't matter," said the patient. Then, in a different voice:

"It doesn't matter. They're a superior intelligence, far beyond our petty imaginations. The ancients knew them but we've forgotten. They're going to return, though. Now that we need them again. They're coming back, to bring us world peace, and universal brotherhood, the government of love. Everyone speaking Esperanto and eating natural foods, and no one wearing any clothes. No more vaccination.

"But, but we're not ready for their gift of peace, not yet. We have to take the sword first. The sword of punishment, piercing us through and through, letting the light into our black souls. Till we're pierced through with the fire, the fire, the fire, the light, the starlight, the stigmata, the pierced windows of cathedrals, pierced like hearts, like saints, like IBM cards, like dead leaves, like dead butterflies, pierced—

"By the nail, the sword, the screw, the dagger, the arrow, the sperm, the needle, the claw, the pin, the quill, quarrel, the fork, the shrill bell, the shot, the dart, the staple, the ruby light, the lightning. The lightning."

He smiled broadly, then winced and put a finger to his lower lip, bringing away a print of smudged blood.

"Dry lips," he apologized. Ointment should be applied.

The doctor sat alone in the room and laughed until he hiccupped. To the intercom:

"Doris, give me a few—heep—minutes and then send in Mr—hup—Mr Griver."

No answer. The receptionist's telephone was ringing, and no one answering that.

"Doris?"

No one was coughing in the waiting room.

Doctors also live inside fragile bodies, with surfaces exposed to wind, grit, bacteria, chafing clothes, invisible dangers, rays from every direction, unseen spores, ridicule, the crossfire of assassins. Most medical men cure this fear by thinking of poor, hateful Edhulme, his corns, his halitosis. Failing a self-cure, a doctor may be struck off the Medical Register. A line is drawn through his name. His patients and his Doris vanish; he himself becomes a "black hole".

Black holes are not, however, empty. Every black hole is actually crammed with an intense presence. Astronomers now believe that black holes are neurotic: They may be calling out to us, saying *hello*, or even *help*. But of course we can never receive their possible communications.

There was no one in the waiting room, no one behind the reception desk. The doctor found Doris and his patients outside, looking at a man who lay in the street. Edhulme had been run down by a lorry.

A dirty day, but real. Edhulme lay trembling by the wheel of the lorry. There were sculpted clumps of dried mud scattered around him, as though he'd burst from a mould. No, of course the mud had fallen from the vehicle's mudguard, which had struck him. The doctor scraped a spot clean with his foot, then knelt to examine the patient.

"Don't try to move, Mr Edhulme. Just take it easy."

The patient made no deliberate move or sound. He wore a cheap, dark-brown suit, a shirt with small brown-and-white checks, frayed at the collar, and a green knit tie. One of his brown scuffed shoes had come off, showing a hole in the toe of his gray wool sock. Adding to his generally old-fashioned appearance was the cut of his mud-brown hair: very short at the sides and brushed back from a deep widow's peak. His face was long and sallow, with large pores around the base of the nose.

On the long chin, the tiny Japanese flag of toilet paper fluttered in the breeze. The doctor, when he had finished his examination, tore it away.

"Ouch," murmured the patient, and died.

A policeman helped him to his feet. "Don't take it so hard,

doctor," he said, quietly. "I know you done your best to save him."

"He told me what happened, constable. It seems he was crossing the road when his leg suddenly went to sleep. Pins and needles. He simply keeled over in front of it."

"Right," said the driver. "He fell right in front of me. What could I do?"

Old Mrs Chatterhand seemed to want to add something, but all she finally said was, "Or or or or or."

AFTERWORD

I seem to keep coming back to stories of ordinary folk in everyday surroundings who are nevertheless seized by cosmic whirlwinds. In "The Answer", "The Interstate", "Name: Please Print" and others, I keep harping on this theme. Does this mean I've given up on the idea of free will? Do I believe there is nothing left but great grinding conspiracies, rolling on towards their own conclusions, and crushing all individuals in their path?

Yes and no. Sure, we have military-industrial complexes, self-serving governments, multinational corporations and uncaring bureaucracies, but not everyone gets downright paranoiac about them. Some people still manage to believe in love, peace, progress, roots, various gods and virtues. Not everyone succumbs to cynicism, despair or paranoia. Bakers continue baking tomorrow's bread.

My own small ray of hope concerns human frailty. All conspiracies, no matter how monstrous, are ultimately the work of mere imperfect people, whose irresolution or bad judgement or even bad conscience works against the system. They get bunions, their cars break down, their children run away—and all this grit gets into the smooth-running gears of their world domination plans. I hope.

Fables

The Snails Who Wanted a King

The snails, discontented with their free and easy life, held a noisy meeting to petition Jupiter for a king.

"We're not complaining," they insisted. "We're very grateful for our portable homes and all. Only we really would like a strong leader. After all, the men have their presidents and showbiz personalities. And you did give the frogs a stork to follow. So how about us?"

Jupiter threw an old log down into their pool and said, "There is a king for you!"

The old log has proved a wise and compassionate leader. Under his guidance, the snails have prospered: now they are seen in all the best restaurants.

Moral: Jupiter, the largest planet in the solar system, has a mass 318 times that of Earth.

The Fox and the Crocodile

A fox was sleeping on the riverbank when up swam a huge crocodile and seized him. He awoke to find hundreds of sharp teeth digging into his belly and back, and the round, rolling eyes of the crocodile looking at him.

"I see I've finally caught you," said the fox.

"What do you mean, *you've caught me?*" The crocodile spoke through hundreds of clenched teeth. You mean *I've caught you.*"

"Don't try to weasel out of it," said the fox. "I've got your jaws locked tight around me, and there's no escape for you now. I figure you're good for about ten pairs of shoes." The crocodile replied, "You must be nuts! I can let go of you anytime I want. Like this, see?"

He opened his jaws and the fox escaped.

Moral: Foxes are probably very sour anyway.

The Three Pigs

One day at the sausage factory, just as a worker was about to slaughter an old sow, one of her ears turned into a silk purse. He rubbed his eyes in disbelief, and sure enough, he was wrong. Back to work.

That night he told his wife about it.

"Oh don't be stupid. Everybody knows you can't make a silk purse out of a sow's ear."

"I didn't make it. I didn't make nothing, it just changed all by itself."

She refused to discuss it any further.

Next day, as he was about to kill another sow, both her ears turned into silk purses. Dropping his pole-axe and knife, the man called one of his co-workers over to see this miracle. But when the other man turned to look, the wily old sow gave a twitch to her two silk purses, and they became ears again.

"Oh did they?" said his wife that night. "You wouldn't even know a silk purse if you saw one. What did they look like?"

He tried to draw her a sketch, but it looked exactly like a sow's ear.

On the third day, a third sow came his way. As he prepared to kill her, both her ears turned into silk purses, and her tail became a golden corkscrew. She was elegant leather all over, like a large football, with a golden zipper down her belly. Before she could change her mind, the man quickly killed her and opened the zipper.

The animal was stuffed with diamonds, rubies, and gold-plated retractable ball-point pens. Excited, the man ran to tell his foreman. But the pig fell back on the conveyor in his absence, and someone in the skinning department became a rich man.

Moral: He who kills quickly and cleanly is not always awarded the ears and tail.

The Dead Pigeon

The emu, the Great Auk, and the passenger pigeon were arguing about life.

"Life?" said the emu. "Don't tell me about life. You just try being Australian, and having three toes, and getting your name in crossword puzzles all the time. That's what life is."

The Great Auk dropped a herring. "I beg to differ. Life is an impenetrable mystery, an enigma wrapped in a conundrum cloaked with dark-shrouded—"

"Who cares?" said the passenger pigeon. "We'll all be as extinct as minks in a few years anyway. Life is getting all you can right now." So saying, he snatched up the herring and tried to gulp it down. When he had strangled to death, the other two shook their heads.

"Last of his kind, wasn't he?"

"I think he had a wife but they weren't living together."

Moral: Extinction is just a different kind of life.

AFTERWORD

Anyone who writes a fable nowadays has plenty of hubris and cheek. After all, the writer is inviting comparison with the giants Aesop and James Thurber. Beside "The Fox and the Crow" or "The Moth and the Star", no run-of-the-mill fable is going to sparkle.

I wrote these, however, when I was younger and more brash. My hubris vanished as soon as they were finished, and I never tried to publish them until now.

On to proverbs.

Ursa Minor

This story begins in complete darkness. First there is the darkness of a London street during a temporary power failure, one rainy night in December. Next there is the wet, patent-leather color of a taxi gliding through the darkness, and next there is the deeper gloom of its interior, where a man, Richard Matlock, sits clutching a teddy bear. He knows nothing of the night or the taxi or the object in his hands. It is his mind that is the complete darkness.

All that Matlock would be able to recall of this evening would be the office party: feeling sick, opening a door to see two figures grappling on top of a drawing table. . . .

"Sorry, sorry." He closed the door again and leaned on the handle for support. There was no way of shutting out the bright glare, the hard, chaotic music, the writhing mob of people wearing silly hats and silly grins. All it meant to them, booze and silly hats. He hadn't even bought Jimmy's present, they couldn't even understand that.

"Would you?" He spoke to the nearest hat, a policeman's helmet, size one. "You bloody wouldn't understand."

"I bloody would," said the hat's owner, an accountant named Ferris. "Happy Christmas!"

"That's the point, see? Christmas is the whole point."

"Right. You couldn't be more right." Ferris hoisted a plastic cup. "Drink to that, all right."

"Right. Man wants to buy a bloody present for his son—his only begotten son—and what happens? Whole world wants to stop him."

"Stop who?"

"Me. You want to stop me, right?"

Ferris stopped grinning. "Hold on now. You say *I* want to stop *you* buying a present for Jesus?"

"No, for *Jimmy*. Jimmy's the name, childhood's the game.

You couldn't care less if he got nothing for Christmas, could you?"

"Matlock, what the hell are you on about? If you want to buy your kid a present—if you want to buy him three presents—far be it from me to—I mean, just go and do it."

"Can't. Too late, shops are shut." Tears welled up in Matlock's eyes. He let go of his drink and took a swing at Ferris, only Ferris was gone; even as his fist cracked the wall he glimpsed the police helmet across the room, bobbing with the music.

"Matlock, isn't it?" Someone took his arm. "Tell you what, let's step outside for a breath of air. You'll feel better."

Matlock pulled away and lurched out the door alone. Somehow he got down the stairs and out into the cold night air. Inside the car-coat he was drenched with sweat, his clothes sticking to him. He waved down a taxi.

"Yes? Where to, mate?"

Jimmy's present. Matlock's watch said 9:01 as he climbed into the taxi. He seemed to be climbing into a dark tunnel, at the other end of which might be what he was looking for.

At the end of the tunnel was Christmas morning. He came awake dreaming, imagining that someone was trying to force his head into a size one police helmet; as he opened his eyes, the torture became a headache. Joan stood over him, holding out a glass of something fizzy.

"Here, take your medicine like a spoilt child."

He sat up and groaned. "I guess I've really done it this time."

"Happy Christmas anyway." She watched him drink the stuff. "I'll admit I was put out, having to pay the taxi driver all that money, just to deliver a mess like you."

"That bad, was I?"

"Not really. All the same, I'm glad you only have office parties once a year. And at least you did remember Jimmy's present."

"Oh—that. Um, and did he like it?"

"He's smitten with it. Carries it about everywhere. Even wanted to share his cereal with it."

Matlock was mystified. For a moment he wondered if drunken

sentimentality hadn't led him to buy a puppy: Say, a furry little ball that would quickly grow into a great, hungry, bad-tempered alsatian.

Joan said, "So it's a success, even if it is a bit motheaten."

"Motheaten, eh."

"Still, it's a nice traditional brown, nothing like the electric pink and blue things they make nowadays. I suppose it's almost an antique. The original Pooh or something. There was a rusty old name tag on the collar. *Daniel, seven*, it said. I took it off and put it away, figuring that if Jimmy ever grows out of teddy bears, we could put the tag back on it and sell it. The beaded collar's nice. Too bad about the frayed ear."

"Ah." He found he could remember nothing of the presumed teddy bear, not even the frayed ear. He was about to say so when there were two sounds: A door slammed, and Jimmy screamed.

They rushed down to the living room to find him dancing up and down, shaking his hand.

"Teddy did it, Daddy! Teddy did it!"

Matlock held him. The damage was slight, a tiny pinch mark. When Jimmy was calm enough he admitted that he'd caught his hand in the door. Somehow he felt Teddy was to blame.

"Don't be silly, now. Teddy's only a little teddy, now, isn't he? He couldn't slam a big door like that."

"No."

"Well, then maybe it was the wind—or maybe a big boy like Jimmy? It just couldn't be Teddy."

Jimmy giggled; a family joke was born. It was Teddy who didn't want to go up for an afternoon nap, Teddy who hated carrots, Teddy who left the water running in the washbasin after Jimmy had brushed his teeth.

That night, Matlock tucked Jimmy and his new pal into bed and told them the story of Goldilocks. It had been Jimmy's favorite story, so now of course Teddy liked it too.

"Somebody's been sleeping in my bed," Matlock intoned in the voice of Papa Bear.

Jimmy chuckled. "Teddy's sleeping in my bed, isn't he, Daddy?"

"That's right. You've both had a long day, and you must be sleepy. So——"

"We saw bears on telly, didn't we? They're big, Daddy."

"Oh yes, the circus."

"Yeah, they were on roller skates. And the man was hitting them with a stick. And they went round and round and round, and he hit them and he——"

"It was all in fun," said Matlock. "Really they like the man, because he gives them their dinners."

Finally Jimmy dozed, and Matlock bent to kiss him. As he did so, he thought he saw something out of the corner of his eye, a movement. Had the bear turned its head?

Of course it hadn't; it lay as before, with its blunt snout and red glass eyes pointing to the ceiling. But now, for the first time, really, Matlock had a chance to examine it more closely.

It looked different, unlike any teddy bear he'd ever seen. Maybe the snout wasn't quite as blunt as it should be, or the eyes set just a fraction close together—but for some reason it had a slightly feral expression. Not "the original Pooh" at all, but more like a model of some real animal. Even the frayed ear looked like the evidence of some old fight.

No, no, it was a stuffed doll and nothing else, and he stared at it until all the strangeness drained away.

"You were a long time," said Joan, downstairs. "Wouldn't he settle down?"

"No, and neither would my nerves. Don't say it—I know—hangover."

She nodded towards two glasses on the coffee table. "I've already poured you a little hair of the—Teddy."

"Now don't *you* start. I have an awful feeling we're going to hear of nothing but Teddy for weeks on end."

And so they did. Jimmy carried the little animal everywhere; held it on his lap on his little rocking chair while watching television; held every bite of food up to its black felt nose before eating it himself; sat whispering secrets into its frayed ear; insisted that everyone kiss Teddy goodnight.

Naturally Teddy was blamed for all incidents that might otherwise be blamed on Jimmy. Teddy tracked mud through the living room, lost one of Jimmy's wellingtons in the garden, left the phone off the hook, scribbled with crayon on the expensive wallpaper in the hall. One afternoon Teddy managed to climb on a kitchen stool and pull a canister of sugar off a high shelf, spilling it all over the floor (and over Jimmy's hair).

Though they ignored most of this, the Matlocks couldn't help picking up Jimmy's family joke. When Joan mislaid a ring, "Teddy must have taken it." It was Teddy who jogged her elbow the time she dropped and broke the steam iron. It was Teddy who stole the key to the basement (where Matlock spent spare hours refinishing old furniture), and when Matlock forgot to pay a bill or found a light bulb burnt out, the little bear was somehow always at the bottom of it. Hardly a day went by without Joan wondering, "Where's Teddy put my change purse this time?" or Matlock muttering that the market looked teddy-bearish. . . .

One night, long after the joke had worn into a habit, Joan and Richard awoke to the smell of smoke.

"You've left something going in an ashtray," she suggested.

"I hope it's only that." He put on the light and searched the room. "Nothing in here, anyway. You take the upstairs, I'll take the down."

The smell lingered long enough for both of them to become fully awake and slightly panicked, and then abated. When they finally gave up the search and came back to bed, Joan sighed:

"Must have drifted in from outside somewhere."

"Or Teddy's taken to cigars."

"Richard, that's not even funny. Do you realize what time it is? Three o'clock."

And at three the next night, they were awakened by the smell of burning. Again they searched the house, and again found no source. Matlock started to say something about Teddy, but stopped himself.

For two more nights, nothing happened. Then:

"Richard, wake up!"

"What? Oh God, not again." But the smell of smoke was there, stronger than ever.

"You go this time," she said. "I've had enough."

For a moment he toyed with the idea of simply falling back in bed and forgetting it. Then he put on his slippers and opened the bedroom door. The smell was strong, and when he put on the hall light, he could see the haze.

It took only a minute to follow it to the kitchen, where he found the light on and blue smoke boiling out of something on the cooker. A saucepan, enveloped in orange flames.

"Christ!" Matlock rushed forward, switched off the gas and threw water on the mess. When he'd quenched the flames and cooled the pan enough to handle it, he carried it up to Joan.

"Pretty damn careless, wouldn't you say? Another half hour, and we'd all be burnt like this. What is it, anyway?"

"I didn't leave anything cooking," she said. "I'm not exactly feeble-minded, you know." She scratched experimentally at the burnt muck in the pan. "My God—it's dry porridge oats."

Later they questioned Jimmy about it, but he seemed genuinely unaware of the incident. Matlock could find no explanation but sleep-walking, and even that sounded a bit too fantastic. Finally they could only put it down to Teddy.

The following night, Matlock heard a loud clatter downstairs. He rushed down to find the kitchen light on, as before. A saucepan lid lay in the middle of the floor, but there was no other sign of disturbance. After checking the doors and windows (locked) and looking in on Jimmy (asleep, so far as he could tell by the dim glow of the nightlight), Matlock went back to bed.

But not to sleep, for a long while. It was an odd little problem: Jimmy couldn't possibly have gone down there, clattered the lid, and sneaked up again without being seen. All right, then, the lid was dropped earlier, and what had awakened Matlock was only the memory of the noise. *If a tree falls in the forest, and there's no one to hear it, does it make a sound?* But the bears hear it. . . . Bears, that could be the answer . . . wean Jimmy from the toy, get him interested in real bears . . . reality, that was the answer. . . .

"Jimmy, I know you like to pretend," he said at breakfast.

The boy stopped feeding Teddy for a moment and looked at him.

"I mean, the story of Goldilocks——"

"And the three bears, Daddy."

"Do you like that story?"

"Yeah."

"But it's only pretend, isn't it? Only a story."

"Daddy——"

"And you like to pretend that Teddy's a real, live bear. Only you and I know that it's just pretend, don't we? We know that Teddy's only a little toy——"

"Excuse me, Daddy. I have to take Teddy to the toilet now."

That evening, Matlock decided to show Jimmy the "real bear" in the basement. Among the accumulated junk furniture awaiting his attempts at restoration were other items picked up at jumble sales and auctions: a nested set of trunks, a parrot cage, a dusty mirror or two, and a bearskin rug. After beating dust from the rug, he draped it over his workbench, then brought Jimmy (and Teddy) down to see it.

Jimmy said nothing for a moment, but stared at the arching red mouth, the white teeth, the clear eyes.

"That, Jimmy, is what a real bear looks like. What do you think of him?"

"Got lots of teeth," said Jimmy quietly. "Does he bite people?"

"Not any more, because he's dead." The word somehow gagged Matlock; he had to swallow and breathe deeply before he could go on. "He's just an old bearskin rug, now."

"Did you kill him, Daddy? I heard you hitting him with a stick."

The conversation wasn't going exactly as Matlock had planned. He felt slightly sick, perhaps from inhaling the dust of the old rug. "Never mind that now. I want you to look at this real bear and then look at Teddy. See the difference? Of course you do. This is a real bear, and Teddy is only pretend."

He seized Jimmy's hand and started to pull him towards the stairs. Jimmy resisted for a second, held and looked back. "He's not so real. If he's so real, why don't he eat everybody up?"

"Come on, will you? Rugs don't eat people, that's why."

As they started up the stairs, Jimmy said, "Well, Teddy's not a rug."

Matlock couldn't sleep. The night-time "incidents" had apparently stopped, but something deeper was still bothering him: at least he assumed it was deeper, since he hadn't the slightest idea what it was.

He went down to the basement, meaning to finish staining a walnut end table. In some way the place felt alien tonight: unearthly quiet, filled with jagged shadows. He shifted the little table about a couple of times, just to hear its legs scrape the concrete floor, and he started humming as he ran his hands over the smooth wood grain. The oppressive stillness seemed to soak up every sound and remain unchanged; he could no more lift the silence than that workbench over there could throw off that heavy, motheaten bear's skin.

What was he looking for? Fine sandpaper, that was it. Yes, to remove that little scratch on the surface. Look at those bear claws, think what they could do to a fine piece of furniture like this.

He wondered why he hadn't packed up the bearskin and put it in one of the trunks. To do it now of course would be pure cowardice, and he was not afraid. But then why was he moving so as not to turn his back on it? Not at all, he was just trying to catch the light right, to see the grain of the wood. Deep in the wood where. . . .

But *that* was the tune he was humming, something about going down in the wood today to be surprised by teddy bears. Bears eating a picnic, was it? A childish tune, sounding just like that other dirge, about the worms crawling in, the worms crawl out . . . and by now he wasn't working at all, just standing there with a sanding block in his hand, staring at the creature.

Its glass eyes stared back. Nothing but dead glass, those, and no doubt the teeth were ivory or plastic. Jimmy was right about that, this bear wasn't "real". The real thing of gristle and bone and power and appetite was gone, probably down the gullets of a few hunters in Canada or wherever. Judging by the age of it, the hunters, too, would be dead and gone; look at the way the moths had been savaging this, making a last meal off the same old bear; look at the condition of that ear, it looked almost . . . frayed.

Only a coincidence, he kept telling himself as he climbed the stairs and slipped into Jimmy's room. Even if it is the same ear, the left or the right, what would that prove? He paused to get his eyes adjusted to the gloom and heard his own heart (. . . teddah . . . teddah . . .).

Jimmy's face lay in shadow, turned from the light. But Teddy's snout and ears were picked out clearly; his red glass eyes were staring at Matlock. No, they were staring *past* Matlock, at something else, something large, dark and formless that stood behind him in the shadows. If he looked, it would be gone, a trick of the imagination. But if he did not look, it would, he knew, come closer.

Matlock reached out, plucked the teddy bear from Jimmy's pillow, and whirled about. There was no great formless being behind him, nothing.

Professor Godber's office at London University was little more than a small cubicle, sparely furnished with a desk, two chairs, a grey filing cabinet. Nothing distinguished it from any other room of business—say, from a police interrogation room—except the curious mask hanging on the wall.

Nor did Professor Godber himself look especially distinguished. No beard, no pince-nez, no mop of wild grey hair, no sober suit or flamboyant cravat. The Professor was young, neat, plain and dressed in a track suit.

"You're lucky to catch me here, Mr Matlock. Term doesn't start till tomorrow, and I should be out in the fresh air while I have the chance. Now what was this all about? Your phone call didn't make it too clear."

Matlock took Teddy from the shopping bag and laid him on the desk. "I don't know—maybe I should be seeing a psychiatrist. I can just imagine it: Telling him 'It's not me that's crazy, doctor. It's this teddy bear.' " He laughed.

Godber waited until he'd stopped, and then said quietly, "I

suppose you saw me on television, talking about magic?"

"Someone at the office did. They said you mentioned something about Red Indians and ghostly bears——"

"The Bear Dance of the Pawnee, that would be. A variant of the Ghost Dance. Do you know anything about the Ghost Dance, Mr Matlock? No? Then let me explain: In the last century, as everyone now knows, white materialism swept across America, and the spiritual culture of the red men was virtually wiped out.

"Now, red men had only spiritual weapons to fight back with—magic, or medicine. Against white men's material science and technology, this was virtually powerless. A major blow came in 1869, when the first transcontinental train went belching and steaming across America. The red prophet Wodziwob saw or heard of this train, and thought about it: what it meant for his people. Then he went up to a mountain where—as prophets have in all ages past—he was given a vision.

"He saw that soon a great catastrophe would strike the whole world. The white men would all be swallowed up, but their houses and their possessions would remain, to be used by the Indians. Finally a spiritual railroad train would steam into view, bearing all of the Indians' greatest ancestors, the ghosts. The most powerful ancestor of all (to some of the many tribes who took up this vision) was the Bear, father and mother and brother and sister of us all."

Professor Godber tapped the teddy bear's snout. "Not much to do with your little friend, here, I'm afraid. Even if his collar does have Indian beads on it." He picked up the bear and turned it, examining the collar. "Hmm, that could be the Pawnee sign for—but then of course there are so many signs quite similar—no, nothing magical about it."

"There used to be a little tag on the collar," said Matlock. "With the former owner's name and age on it. Daniel, seven, it said."

The Professor stared, then smiled. "I see, you're sent here by one of my students, to pull my leg, is that it? Okay, joke's over. You can go home."

"What? No, I—the tag? I have it at home. It was rusty, and it seemed silly to keep a tag with some other kid's name, so——"

"Wait here for a moment. Don't move!" Godber raced out of the room and was back in a minute with two large, dusty volumes. He slapped them on his desk and started paging through one of them so rapidly that it seemed impossible that he should not tear one of the brittle sheets.

"But I don't understand."

"Shh. Ah, here it is: 'The shaman Wynoka claimed to know much of white man's medicine, that is, he knew how to read and write. He took the Bear Dance from the Pawnee to his own tribe, whom he always referred to in ritual language as the Bear People. It is said that he carried always a small image of a bear, given him by a white family who also believed in the Bear Dance. Around its neck he hung a metal disc, inscribed *Daniel, seven*. Wynoka called this totem Little Bear, and he often said, "Little Bear is with us now, but when the white man departs from us, he will go with Great Bear." Wynoka was executed by the 11th Cavalry at Fort Truscott, in 1893, but his "Little Bear" disappeared during the trial, and was never seen again.' " Professor Godber closed the book and smiled at the object on his desk. "Until now. In England. Nearly a hundred years later. Incredible."

After a moment of silence, Professor Godber opened a desk drawer and pulled forth a tape recorder and a jumble of wire. "Now, I want you to go over your whole story for me, Mr Matlock. Very slowly, and in the greatest detail. I want it all."

Two hours later, Matlock thought he had finished. Godber told him he'd probably remember more; later they'd go over it again.

"Okay, but I still don't see exactly how this fits. I mean, what about the burnt porridge?"

"Ah. Well, magic isn't always spelt out and underlined, but I think I see. You mention the story of Goldilocks and the Three Bears, for example. The little white girl goes among the savage beasts—to their home, in fact—and steals from them. She takes their food, their home, even the place where Baby Bear is supposed to lay his head. But isn't that almost an allegory of what white people did to the Bear People in America? They came, stole everything worth stealing in the way of food and land and goods, and—so far as we know—got away with it. Notice that the story of Goldilocks comes to an abrupt end: 'Someone's been sleeping in my bed. And here she is!' Naturally you'd expect the bears to take some revenge, but the story says nothing about it. Could it be we've been telling it wrong, all this time?

"Then there's the curious story of Little Bear here, and Wynoka, the magician who kept him. Notice that Wynoka died in 1893. Within a year or so, nearly all the magicians and prophets who advocated the Ghost Dance had been executed, by the way. But also within a year or so, a white named Teddy Roosevelt returned from the Wild West with a lot of stories about how terrific it was to kill bears. At once people started making little stuffed images of bears, naming them after this white hunter, Teddy. You see? As soon as Little Bear vanishes, copies of Little Bear crop up all over the damned white world! That, my friend, is very powerful medicine indeed."

"So you think this is really an Indian——"

"No, no, you're missing the point. Magic goes much deeper than you or I or the Pawnee or anybody else thinks. Think how peculiar—how other-worldly—bears really are. How magical they've always been. The Celts probably worshipped them, and so did the Persians. Constellations were named after Little Bear and Great Bear long before American Indians played with the idea. They've always been known as Little Bear, a friendly, innocuous chap, and Great Bear, the darkest symbol of death and destruction. Just look at the other names for Ursa Major: the Plough; the Big Dipper (dipping up the waters of life and dashing them down again). And in the Middle Ages they called it the Wain, the hay wagon, and they used to portray it carrying all humanity to Judgement Day, over the motto: 'All flesh is grass'. Death and destruction.

"Yes, we civilized folk have plenty to answer for, chopping up the natural world, forgetting the old myths, trying to cut the bear down to a manageable size. Think of that: our alter ego, powerful, intelligent, indestructible, the very symbol of strength and spirit. We've tried to turn it into Smokey the Bear, and Rupert, and Pooh, Br'er Bear and Paddington and the victims of Goldilocks' little prank; cuddly toys for the kiddies; adverts for breakfast cereals flavored with honey—do you realize, if evolution had taken a slightly different turn, we'd be out there in the wood and the bears would be here eating porridge!

"But now, I think perhaps they're fighting back. Oh, maybe it's not them specifically, but I think some principle of magic is out to restore the terrible imbalance of nature we've created. Think of the yeti, that great hairy 'abominable snowman' everyone sees all over the Himalayas, but no one can catch. He appears, scares the daylights out of people, and then vanishes into thin air. It's much the same with a creature they've recently started seeing deep in the California forests, that they call 'Bigfoot'. Lately similar creatures have been glimpsed in North Dakota, Canada . . . are they 'real' or ghosts? No one can say. And that, Mr Matlock, is the dreadful part of it: our sense of reality itself may be breaking down."

"The final destruction."

"Precisely. One day we may well begin to wonder: Are we bears, dreaming that they're men?"

When Matlock left, taking Teddy, he felt vaguely cheated. All of Professor Godber's fine theories were of no use at all to him. If evil was coming, could he avert it? How? By drawing a pentacle on the kitchen floor? Praying to Ursa Major? Sticking pins in Teddy? Once away from the Professor's office, the whole business sounded quaint and more than a little silly. Godber had no sound, practical advice, psychological or spiritual. The best thing might be to drop Teddy in a litter bin somewhere, buy Jimmy a nice nylon bear in pink and green, and forget all about Bigfoot and Little Bear and the rest of it.

So thinking, Matlock managed to take a wrong turn among the corridors of London University; he entered a courtyard he'd never seen before and crossed to a strange building. Just inside the door was a glass case with a dummy in it: A white, elderly man dressed in nineteenth-century costume and a panama hat, seated comfortably and having no apparent purpose he could imagine.

A uniformed guard said, "That's Jeremy Bentham, sir. The

great Utilitarian. Not a wax model, no sir, it's *him*. Had himself stuffed after he died."

"Stuffed?"

"Yes sir. And every year at the Founder's Day dinner, so I hear, they set him up at table beside everyone else. Never seen it myself."

Matlock was beginning to feel unreal again. He quickly asked directions and left, before he should find himself enquiring whether the stuffed Bentham were fond of porridge.

"So it's a story without an ending?" asked Joan.

"Like Goldilocks, yes."

"Where's Teddy, then?"

"I've disposed of him. Told Jimmy he'd gone on a long voyage, 'where no bear has gone before', and he seemed to take it gracefully. Actually Ted's in the dustbin at the bottom of our garden."

"Is that wise? They say bears are clever at prowling around dustbins."

"Very funny," he said, yawning. "Shall we go up to bed?"

"If no one's been sleeping in it."

The phone rang.

"I'll get it," he said. "You go on up."

It was Professor Godber. "Any developments, Mr Matlock?"

"Not a thing. In fact, I've thrown Teddy away and bought my son a replacement. It's big, 'cute', covered with chartreuse nylon fur, and if you pull a string it says 'I'm Buzzy Bear, and I like you'. What do you say to that?"

"Oh." The Professor sounded crestfallen. "Well I just called to tell you I've solved the riddle of 'Daniel, seven'. At first I thought it might be something to do with Daniel Boone. You know, *Dan'l Boone kilt a b'ar* and all that. But then . . ."

Smiling, Matlock gently put down the receiver. But on second thought, he lifted it again; the Professor was still talking:

". . . because if Wynoka could read, he almost certainly read the Bible. So sure enough, Daniel, chapter seven, goes like this:

Daniel had a dream and visions of his head upon his bed . . . and behold another beast, a second, like unto a bear, and it raised itself on one side, and it had three ribs in the mouth of it between the teeth of it: and they said thus unto it, Arise, devour much flesh."

It was not a bear that plundered the dustbin, but Matlock. The only way to be sure of the ending was total destruction. He carried the teddy bear in to the kitchen, laid it on the table, and then ripped open its belly with a knife.

The masses of hair he pulled forth were faded, but still recognizably golden. He sat staring at them until alerted by a sound: Something was scratching at the basement door.

AFTERWORD

My only attempt to write a ghost story suffers from two flaws that I've noticed. First, there ought to be more physical detail in the family life. Second, there is a decided lack of plausibility in certain parts.

I'm not sure how to cure the implausibility. The odd thing about it is, just those parts that sound least likely are true. The anthropological tale about Ghost Dances and so on sounds phoney, but it is almost wholly factual. Many readers will no doubt reject the idea that at London University the stuffed body of Jeremy Bentham sits in a glass case in the hall. But it's true, I swear it. I've seen the grisly exhibit myself, from about the distance you see this page.

Sinister teddy bears are no new thing in science fiction, of course. Offhand I can think of two examples—Philip K. Dick's "Second Variety" and Harry Harrison's "I Always Do What Teddy Says"—but I'm sure there are more. Some readers may feel that my sinister teddy is following a beaten path, but I prefer to think of it as following a hallowed precedent. It depends on whether one thinks of science fiction as extension or codification, right? Right.

Calling All Gumdrops!

Mommy and Daddy Mason were up in their own room, smoking a cigar and drinking real chocolate milk. Mommy stood by the window, puffing, waving the smoke out through the screen into the summer night. Daddy guarded the door, hunkered down with his back against it and his bare knees sticking up. One knee had a scab.

"It's awful quiet downstairs," he said.

"You think maybe they went out?"

"Maybe. Not that *I* care." Daddy Mason took a big swig of chocolate milk and held up the bottle, as though checking its color. Its color was brown. "Why don't you go down and see?"

"Why don't you?" Mommy laughed as she passed him the cigar. She climbed up on the top bunk and sat kicking her sneakers against the wall. "You wouldn't dare go down there, not in a million years."

"I would so. I'm not afraid of them." He stepped to the window with the cigar. "You think maybe they went out?"

After a minute, Mommy said, "I'm not afraid of them either. I just don't like them, that's all." Her sneaker toes made precise little rubber stamp marks on the wall, right up to the edge of the Superman poster. "I *hate* them."

Daddy looked at her. "I'll tell."

"Okay, maybe I don't hate them, but what do I feel? What am I supposed to feel? I've given them the best years of my life—I tried to give them everything. Where did I go wrong? Maybe I loved them too much. Maybe that's where I failed them, I loved them too much." She had memorized this speech from *Dorinda's Destiny*, a soap opera rich in the raw materials of life. "Life is a whole new ballgame."

In the old ballgame, Mommy Mason had been a public relations coordinator specializing in rodeos and stock car races. One afternoon her boss. Tony Murth, had called her into his office. He was searching through all the drawers of his desk.

"Never can find a dad-blamed thing around here, Linda. I was looking for this here form letter 47B, you know the one? That says an employee is fired."

"Look, Tony, I know a few of my accounts dried up, but——"

"Here it is." He handed her the form letter. "You're fired, Linda."

"It doesn't seem fair. I mean, I'm not the only one."

"Lordy, don't I know? I gotta fire everybody. Only a matter of time before I gotta fire me. Ain't it the shinola, though? Whole durn industry is drying up. Roller derbies, circuses, ice shows, faith healers, carnivals, wrestling—nobody takes nothing serious no more."

"Nobody cares."

"Nobody cares about nothing. If we fixed up to have the President jump a motorcycle over the Capitol building, we might just sell enough tickets to pay for the gas." He began searching through desk drawers again. "Nobody wants to take their kids nowhere no more."

"Maybe it's the kids," she suggested. "They're different these days. They make their own fun. They go off by themselves more, and—but couldn't it be just a fad? And when they get tired of it——"

"We can't run a whole industry on hope. The circus tigers need meat, the cowboys need beans, the wrestlers need Reichian analysis. Nope, kid, this is it. The organized leisure industry is a dead yak." Tony Murth found what he was looking for, a child's pacifier, and popped it between his lips. "There! Helpsh me shtop shmoking."

"But if the kids ever——"

"Kids these days," he murmured, a far-away look in his eyes. "Who understands 'em?"

"That's no argument. People always said that."

"True. True." She waited for more, but Tony Murth merely sat quietly, his eyes unfocused, his mouth now and then twitching at the pacifier.

Unemployment had agreed with Mommy Mason, however. She was a slim, suntanned woman of thirty, with short cropped blonde hair and a smile only slightly marred by her new braces. She wore a striped polo shirt and bib overalls, embroidered on the bib with a popular television dog, Mister Fuzzle. Her sneakers were going to pieces.

Unemployment seemed to agree with Daddy Mason too. He was a lean, suntanned man of thirty, with short cropped dark hair and a smile only slightly marred by a missing incisor. He wore cut-down jeans, a striped T-shirt and running shoes. There was a scab on his knee that he couldn't help picking.

In the old ballgame, he had been a video editor for an educational production company. Education, as usual, meant puppets.

One afternoon his boss, Nora Volens, had called him into her office.

"Nick, you've been doing nice work for us."

"Sounds like you're getting ready to can me, ha ha."

"Ha ha, well not exactly, Nick."

"Ha, not exactly? Nora, what does that mean?"

"The whole company's folding. We're all out of a job."

"Gumdrops!" he exclaimed. "What the sam hill is going on, Nora?"

She began fiddling with the stuffed animal on her desk, a replica of the company's most popular TV puppet, Mister Fuzzle. "Nobody seems to know why, but educational TV is finished. Maybe the kids are going out to play more sandlot ball or something, maybe—maybe the nature of education is changing. Who knows."

"Yeah but that's no answer. Who ever knew?"

She picked up the doll and hugged it. "Anyway, Mister Fuzzle will always have a home with me."

The whole new ballgame began.

Mommy took a swig of chocolate milk and then tried blowing across the top of the bottle to produce a low, melancholy note. Daddy had put out the cigar by rubbing it against the window screen. Now he sat picking at his scab.

"I watched the six o'clock news," she said. "They said the word 'kids' is going out of style in the East. They said it's pejorative, it's parentalist."

"I can see that. But they call us——"

"The younger people now prefer to be called 'junior citizens', and I guess that name is catching on. In the East."

"Criminitly," he said. "They get to call us all kinds of names, if you're unemployed they call you a——"

An even lower note from the bottle. "With sixty per cent hardcore unemployment, you expect them to look up to us?"

"It's as if they were aliens," he said. "Aliens, posing as our children just long enough to take over, I don't know, the world supply of niacin, thiamine and riboflavin."

"Stop picking that scab. How would these aliens get here?"

"Who knows? Flying saucers, funny rays, an invisible gas, the point is, they're just like the aliens in movies—they never want to have any fun."

"Interesting theory," she said. "But hey, if you don't stop picking at that scab, your knee'll get all infected, all pus and blood poisoning. Cripes, they'll probably have to cut your whole leg off!"

"I don't care."

"Gee you're dumb!"

"I am not!"

The argument was interrupted by something rattling against the screen. Mommy went to look out, as more gravel twanged against the wire mesh. Down below, in the streetlight filtering down through a sycamore, she could make out two figures. One wore a hat with mouse ears.

"It's Mommy and Daddy Green," she said, and called down to them in a stage whisper. "Hey you guys, what's happening?"

"Nothing, we're just messing around. Can you get out?"

"Naw, we gotta stay in all week, on account of we didn't do our homework. Our job retraining stuff."

"Don't be a dope, you can just tie some sheets together or something and slide down. Come on, hey."

Daddy Mason said, "I don't know——" But Mommy was

already tying sheets in a square knot, which is stronger, boy, than any knot you can name.

She slid down first. When Daddy Mason followed, he fell and bumped his elbow. He rolled around on the damp grass for a minute, crying, until the others called him a big baby. Then he jumped up and hit Daddy Green in the back.

"Oh yeah?"

"Yeah!" The two men locked arms and wrestled for a minute.

"Come on," said Mommy Green to Mommy Mason. "Let's us just ignore these very immature dumb dopes." They linked arms and walked on until the men came puffing along, now and then trying to shove or trip one another. Before they'd gone another block, a prowl car pulled up and shone its light on them. They heard the power hum of a bullhorn.

"Where are you going, gumdrops?" asked a shrill voice.

"The root beer stand, uh, sir."

"Do your children know where you are?"

"Sure they do."

The light flashed on each of their faces in turn. The voice finally said, "Okay. But remember, there's a curfew." Whoever or whatever was in charge of the car never emerged from behind the black windows at all—just turned off its bullhorn and light and drove away.

The root beer stand, thought Daddy Mason, what a comedown. Time was when they'd have gone to a real bar. But now even people who had the money for real liquor didn't want to drink. Everybody was dieting or else in training or else allergic to smoke. Some didn't like the taste of booze and some couldn't afford it. Anyway, as everybody knew, the bars were all full of very immature people.

The old root beer stand just seemed the natural place to hang out now. A frosty mug of root beer only cost a nickel, and you could hang out all evening, just fooling around. There were yellow fluorescent tubes along the eaves of the ramshackle old place, and June bugs were always zooming in on these to crash against the weathered clapboard. You could sit at a shadowy, rough old picnic table and slap mosquitoes and listen to crickets and watch the moths and June bugs. In the summer night, you were in a world of insects.

Tonight there were lots of other gumdrops here: some on their way home from swimming, their suits rolled up in soggy towels and their wet hair slicked back. Some on bikes or roller skates, moving and weaving among the tables.

Tonight was different. People seemed excited for no good reason. There was plenty of noise, shouting and laughing. Some of the Daddies bellowed at each other, pounded their chests and yodelled. Some of the Mommies kept getting the giggles.

Daddy Taylor, a big man wearing a beanie covered with buttons and bottle caps, was the cause of it all. As soon as the Masons and Greens sat down with their root beer, he lurched over and poured something into it out of a square bottle.

"Hey is that booze? Cause I don't drink, see, I——" Daddy Mason began.

"You drink with me," said Daddy Taylor. He was big and in good condition. Everybody drank with him. "'At's it," he said, waving the bottle. "Plenty more where this comes from. Pulenty. *And*——" He staggered away without finding a finish to the thought. After a couple of drinks, they no longer minded his bullying.

"Kids," said Daddy Green. "Who understands 'em? My kids, my own kids are like——"

"Like aliens," said Daddy Mason. "I know."

"Like robots, I was gonna say. Like gosh-darned robots!"

"Or aliens."

"Like gosh-darned robots, like machines, they don't ever have any fun. They don't know what fun is. They go to school. Then they go to their after-school jobs. Then they come home, eat——"

"Robots don't eat, hey. But aliens——"

"Shut up, will you? Whose kids are they, anyway?"

"Yeah, but aliens might——"

"Just shut up. They eat, then they do their homework, fool around with the computer or just read, now and then go to scout meetings. Then they brush their teeth and go to bed. Just like robots, like——"

"Or aliens."

A woman spoke up. "I don't think there's anything wrong with the children. I think it's us, there's something wrong with us. I mean just look at us, the way we——" The rest was lost in booing and shouting, until Daddy Taylor told them all to shut their faces.

"Criminy!" he boomed. "We all got a right to speak our piece here. Heck, that's the whole point, I didn't bring a case of gin down here just to make everybody sick. Heck, I know—we all know—something is sure wrong somewheres, us gumdrops are getting a raw deal. Right? So if we all speak our piece, maybe—I don't know, maybe——"

Mommy Mason said, "I don't think the kids are aliens or robots, but I don't think it's us, either. It's—I don't know, the kids are like, like zombies. I mean, they're still our kids, but they just—I don't know."

"We're the zombies," said the woman who'd spoken before. "We're the ones turning into bodies without heads, we're the damned zombies!"

"Hey, she swore! She cussed!" someone shouted over the general uproar. Mommies and Daddies were jumping up and shouting swear words all over the place.

Daddy Mason felt someone slip something into his hand. It was a note. He opened it under the table, where there was just enough light to make it out.

I THINK YR KIND A CUTE!!!

He looked up and saw Mommy Green smiling at him. She winked. He tried winking back, but the other eye kept closing too.

Daddy Taylor pounded his mug on the table. "Okay, you guys, we all agree there's something wrong with the kids or with us or with everybody. You wanta hear what I think? I think the machines are taking over, using the kids to run everything. The kids and the computers are working together to—to make slaves out of us!"

"Yeah but hey——"

"They boss us every minute of the god-durn day! We have to take out the trash, and wash the dishes, and do everything they say, or we don't get our allowances. Am I right? Am I right?"

There was a hearty cheer, then applause, whistles.

"You all know I'm right. So what are we gonna do? Are we gonna sit around and let them take over our world? Or are we gonna fight! fight! fight!"

People were jumping up and down on the tables. A man in a propellor beanie waved a revolver in the air. "I got my piece!" he bellowed, his props spinning wildly. "You all get yours! Let's fight! Let's fight! Let's fight! Let's fight!"

"Fight who?" Daddy Mason murmured, unable to hear his own voice in the noise. He felt awful, his head spinning so that he couldn't do the one thing he wanted to do, which was to remember Mommy Green's first name.

"All right, gumdrops, break it up. Curfew time," said a shrill, amplified voice. The prowl car played its light over them like a cold hose, and for a moment it seemed as if they would slink away, sobered and scared.

Then someone threw a rock. "Fight! Fight! Fight! Fight!" People were rushing forward, and Daddy Mason found his rubbery legs carrying him forward too. Everyone got hold of the sleek dark car and pulled and pushed until it started rocking. The spotlight twisted back and forth uselessly until someone smashed it with a rock. Then, without a further word of protest, the prowl car went over.

"Wahoo!"

Everything else was a blur. He ran through strange, dark streets on his rubbery legs, and other gumdrops ran with him. Where to? Wahoo!

Mommy Mason at first stuck close to the big guy, Daddy Taylor, the only one who seemed to know what was going on. He also knew the guy who turned up with a big box of weapons and was passing them out: pistols, rifles, shotguns, bayonets, knives and axes, baseball bats. If there was going to be that kind of trouble, she wanted a weapon of her own. She chose a revolver, examined it, and started to give it back.

"This is only a starting pistol."

Daddy Taylor grinned. "They all are, but keep it. The enemy won't know you're firing blanks."

The man with the propellor beanie looked apologetic. "All our stuff is junk, not much ammo. What we shoulda had was machine guns, grenades, mines, rockets. Even a Colt .45 automatic, boy with that you can knock anybody right on their behind!"

Mommy Mason found she was dizzy, so she leaned against Daddy Taylor's muscles. "I hope nobody minds my asking, but just who the hell are we supposed to be shooting at? I mean so far all I heard was about kids and computers—you wanta go shooting little kids? No, I thought not. So that leaves computers? You want me to fire blanks at a computer?"

Daddy Taylor seemed very annoyed. "Look, if we don't all stick together we don't get nowheres," he said, shoving her away. "If you don't wanta fight, you can do some reconnaissance, okay? We need people to look in some windows and *find out what they're up to.*"

"Yeah," said the man with the propellor beanie. He pointed to a distant home. "That's my place, you could start there. Find out what my kids are doing."

The booze was firing her up to say something mightily sarcastic. Then she caught the look in the propellor man's eyes—frightened, pleading. She nodded and set off, jogging on wobbly legs. Within minutes she'd found a window.

She could see three kids facing one corner of the room, evidently watching the TV news. A boy and a girl around ten years old, and another boy about five. Their zombie-like, robot-like, alien faces took in everything without changing expression.

Mommy Mason could hear the sounds of crashing glass and shouting on the TV, which said: ". . . street where the rioters turned to looting. Things were more serious across the river, where a mob broke into the armory and emerged with mines, rockets, grenades and guns. But *don't be scared*, kids. Things will settle down before morning, you'll see."

"But why?" asked one of the older kids. "The gumdrops

have got everything they need or want. Why this?"

The TV said, "Well, Jimmy, that's a big question, and we'd all like a lot more answers here. It has to do with today's social structure and how it came about. You know we went into that before: How once there were grownups who did all the work and earned all the money and took care of the kids, remember? And then there was a lot of what we called family role slippage in the 1950s, wasn't there?"

One of the kids said, "Yeah, there was some kind of big war that split up a lot of families in funny ways. Kids were raising themselves more."

"That's right, Sally," said the TV. "Kids took after-school jobs, they dated earlier. They were expected to imitate grownups. Grownups, meanwhile, were getting much more interested in what they called *leisure activities*, or playing. In the 1950s they went bowling, they went water skiing, they relaxed in bermuda shorts while listening to 45 rpm records of Perry Como. The idea was that leisure was for relaxing, resting from their labors.

"In the 1960s the grownups played with sex and drugs—we haven't gone into those yet, we'll discuss them later—and music and pretty clothes to dress up in. Now they didn't want to relax, they wanted to be childlike and innocent.

"In the 1970s grownups wore kids' clothes, playsuits and running shoes, and they went hang-gliding and roller-skating when they weren't reading comics or going to movies like *Popeye* and *Superman*. They worked very hard at being kids. All they had to do was lose their jobs. The 1980s and 1990s took care of that, through automation. *Grownups* gave up, they became *gumdrops*."

"It's not fair!" said the little boy.

"No, Billy, but it's nobody's fault, either. Until we can get gumdrops interested in adulthood, we'll just have to carry on ourselves. We computers and you junior citizens are in charge, for now."

Mommy Mason heard something in Jimmy's voice, when he said, "It's so hard. You get so tired sometimes . . ." She stared at the children, whose cheeks were wet. Imagine that, crying over a boring old bunch of history!

Daddy Mason found he was sitting in a funny little house. For some reason, Mommy Green was there, too. They sat on little chairs, staring out the window at the night sky. Somewhere a magazine had exploded, and there were rockets and tracers, bombs and flares, scribbles of light on the blackness.

"Where are we?" he asked.

"In our back yard, Nick. This is our playhouse. Like it?"

"Great." Janice, that was her name. "Great, Janice."

"I like you," she said, putting her hand on his bare knee.

"I like you too. Watch out for the scab."

"Oh." She took her hand away, but continued smiling at him. Daddy Mason wondered whether they ought to maybe kiss or something.

After a moment, they turned away from one another and stared at the fireworks outside. From time to time, there would be a brilliant flash of light or a loud bang, and Daddy Mason would say:

"Boy, somebody's in trouble!"

"Yes," she'd say. "Yeah." She peered hard into the darkness, the scribbles of light, as though trying to see there some written explanation of her feelings.

"If you keep scratching at a scab," Daddy Mason said, "you can get a lot of pus and blood poisoning."

AFTERWORD

The juvenility of adults is naturally more apparent to someone moving on through middle age, to whom most adults are relatively young in fact. But I see adults my own age dressing in children's sports clothes, reading comics and going to Rocky *movies. A friend of mine (who had not read this story) recently explained the vigorous litigiousness of today's Americans in the same way. People sue each other over everything because, like children, they can never take any responsibility for their own lives. Someone else has to be blamed.*

My four-year-old daughter is the same. Whenever she finds out that anything is broken, she immediately wants to know who *broke it. Affixing blame is one of the great pastimes of childhood. I remember long arguments about whether someone was safe or out, about who pushed whom first, and so on.*

Excuse me, I hear an ice-cream van. I'll just go get a 99 and then if nobody wants to play catch, I'll go back to work on my model airplane.